He walked toward her, each step closer upping his desire.

His fingertips burned at the memory of how hot her bare skin had been beneath his touch. Excitement and lust heightened his senses as he stopped just a couple feet from her. That floral scent, soft and feminine, teased him, drew him nearer as he leaned down.

"What did you want to talk about?" he whispered into her ear.

Calandra's head snapped up and she turned, her mouth so close to his that all he'd have to do was lean forward and claim her.

Her lips parted. He leaned in, ready to kiss her.

"Your child."

The words hung in the air. He drew back and stared down at her. He'd heard the words, knew they'd been spoken, but couldn't fully comprehend.

"I'm... My what?"

Her fingers came up and clenched the pendant around her neck so tight that her knuckles turned white. "Your child, Alejandro. I'm pregnant."

The Infamous Cabrera Brothers

They're undeniably tempting...and unexpectedly tempted!

One's brooding, one's scandalous, one's mysterious...

Everyone knows who the Cabrera brothers are. Their billion-dollar business ventures have put them on the map and their devilishly handsome looks turn heads the world over.

But truly getting to know the tall, dark and Spanish bachelors? That's something only three exceptional women will have the pleasure of...

Discover Adrian's story in
His Billion-Dollar Takeover Temptation

Read Alejandro's story in
Proof of Their One Hot Night

Both available now!

And look out for Antonio's story

Coming soon!

Emmy Grayson

PROOF OF THEIR ONE
HOT NIGHT

HARLEQUIN
PRESENTS

Recycling programs
for this product may
not exist in your area.

ISBN-13: 978-1-335-56806-9

Proof of Their One Hot Night

Copyright © 2021 by Emmy Grayson

Harlequin Enterprises ULC
22 Adelaide St. West, 40th Floor
Toronto, Ontario M5H 4E3, Canada
www.Harlequin.com

Printed in U.S.A.

Emmy Grayson wrote her first book at the age of seven about a spooky ghost. Her passion for romance novels began a few years later with the discovery of a worn copy of Kathleen Woodiwiss's *A Rose in Winter* buried on her mother's bookshelf. She lives in the Midwest countryside with her husband (who's also her ex-husband), their baby boy and enough animals to start their own zoo.

Books by Emmy Grayson

Harlequin Presents

His Billion-Dollar Takeover Temptation

Visit the Author Profile page
at Harlequin.com for more titles.

To my editor, Charlotte. I'm a better writer because of you.

To my husband and my mother. Book two is possible because of you.

To my Thursday night critique group. For believing in me and loving me.

To my son. Baby Boy, you're our world.

CHAPTER ONE

CALANDRA SMYTHE'S EYES flew open as a warm, muscled arm curled around her stomach. She met her own gaze in the mirror above the bed and barely bit back a gasp.

Midnight-blue silk covered her chest and hips, but beneath the covers she was most definitely nude, the fabric a cool kiss against her bare skin. Her hair, which she normally kept contained in a bun, flared out in dark brown waves across her pillow. Lips swollen, cheeks tinged pink…

Oh, no. She looked like she belonged on the cover of a romance novel.

So did the naked man with his arm across her belly. His face was buried in his pillow, but his bare backside was on full display in the mirror. Dark hair curled across the nape of his neck; he had broad shoulders and a muscular back that begged for a woman's fingers to glide over every ridge before trailing lower…

Stop!

Slowly, Calandra got her racing heartbeat back under control. How the hell could she have let this happen? She never did anything this impulsive. Never let anyone get too close. But last night it was like someone else had taken over her body, made her respond with a smile and a flirtatious laugh instead of the cold stare she usually leveled at people who bothered her. If her boss found out what she'd done, or in this case *whom* she'd done, the career she'd fought tooth and nail for would be gone.

Sunlight streamed through the blinds and hit her square in the eyes. Squinting against the brightness, she managed to wiggle out from under the heat of her lover's arm and swing her legs over the edge of the bed. Her feet sank into the plush rug, belying the ache between her thighs. A marble fireplace dominated one side of the room, while a row of windows provided an incredible view of the sun rising over the Hudson River.

Once, a long time ago, she'd been surrounded by opulence like this. Endless toys, designer clothes, trips to France and Italy and Turkey.

She'd been miserable.

But easier to focus on the luxury than the stark-naked man sleeping peacefully behind her. Easier to evaluate details like the spa tub she glimpsed through the bathroom door than to recall the feel of lips trailing over her neck, her breasts, her stomach, leaving sparks of fire burning across her skin. To face the realization that she'd finally given up her virginity to a man whose company she'd despised for the past three years.

She grabbed her phone off the table and stifled a gasp. Six thirty in the morning? She hadn't slept past four in years.

A delicious shiver danced down her spine. Given how energetic their bed play had been, it shouldn't surprise her that she'd overslept.

Fortunately, there were no missed calls or texts from

Adrian. No matter how incredible the night had been, no experience was worth risking her reputation.

Or her heart. She prided herself on her ability to keep everyone at arm's length. Indulging in a night of sex had never been worth testing that ability.

Until a night had suddenly seemed worth it. A night of incredible, mind-blowing, soul-stirring sex.

A quick glance over her shoulder verified that he was still sleeping. Sunshine fell upon his back, casting a golden glow over his chiseled muscles. Muscles that had sent a thrill through her veins as her fingers explored every inch of him.

Enough of that.

She turned away and stood. Where had her evening gown ended up? She needed to get dressed and get out of the suite before—

"*Buenos días,* Callie."

Alejandro Cabrera grinned as Calandra froze, her stunning body backlit by the morning sun. The light caressed her toned frame, from the delicateness of her swan-like neck to those long, long legs. Perhaps he could persuade her to join him back in bed and kiss his way up from the slender curve of her calves to those luscious lips, with some detours along the way.

Although judging by the tense set of her shoulders and the alarm in her gray eyes, a repeat of last night's performance wasn't happening anytime soon.

Too bad. The cold-blooded event manager with a heart of ice that he normally dealt with had thawed and revealed an enticing woman who had intoxicated him with heady kisses and passionate moans as he explored every inch of her supple body.

Her virgin body. That had been an unexpected shock. Yet it had filled him with a possessiveness he'd never experienced, one that had made him an even more attentive and gentle lover.

Although their second round had not been gentle. Calandra had responded with a passion that brought him to new heights of pleasure. Heights, he thought with a grin, he was more than happy to revisit.

He sat up and leaned against the headboard. Calandra's gaze flickered down to his groin. Just a glance made him stir. Two spots of red appeared in her cheeks, and she looked away.

His grin widened. "Nothing you haven't seen before."

A grimace passed over her face. "Please don't remind me."

Not the first thing women usually responded with after sharing his bed. He frowned. Had he imagined the passionate temptress in his bed last night? Or worse, had he not been gentle enough? Her virginity had surprised him, but when he'd tried to pause, she'd grabbed his hips and pulled him deep with such demand he'd nearly embarrassed himself.

Before he could say anything else, she darted across the room and scooped her dress off the floor. She fumbled with the soft material before it slipped from her fingers and pooled in a black satin heap at her feet. She stared at it for a moment, as if willing the dress to levitate off the ground and cover her. Then, with a quick breath, she raised her chin and looked right at him.

There. The tiniest fire flickered in her eyes, smoky and defiant. Standing there in all her bare glory, hair unbound and falling in tousled waves over her alabaster shoulders, she looked like a dark-haired version of Aphrodite rising from the black folds of a stormy sea.

"Stop staring."

He tore his gaze away from the rose-colored tips of her breasts and refocused on her eyes.

Her flat, emotionless gray eyes. Something twisted in his chest. He missed the spark that had flickered to life just last night, then flamed into a blazing inferno as they'd left the empty ballroom behind.

Now that he'd glimpsed the real Calandra, he didn't want her to retreat back into the detached professional he'd come to know.

Not that it mattered, he reminded himself. He'd be on a plane to New Orleans this afternoon. Calandra would return to her career as event planner for his brother's company, Cabrera Wines. And their one night of passion, no matter how intensely pleasurable it had been, would gradually fade as time passed and new women graced his bed.

He covered his momentary lapse into maudlin territory with his customary playboy smile.

"Nothing I haven't seen already."

"Now, Alejandro."

With a disappointed sigh, he averted his gaze and stared out the windows at the towers of New York City sparkling in the early-morning light. He hadn't planned on dropping in for the release party of his brother's latest wine. But *maldición*, he was glad he had. It had been a solid month since he'd pleasured a woman. As much as he enjoyed teasing Calandra, he never would have guessed that she would be his next lover.

Or that she'd be untouched. Possession wound itself through his veins, hot and…desperate. Desperate to keep her all to himself, to not let anyone see the treasure that had been lurking beneath her dark clothing and stern expression.

A discreet glance over his shoulder made his chest tighten as he took in the sensual curve of her back, her tapered waist and those gorgeous legs disappearing into her dress.

Yes. Definitely glad.

"Well."

He suppressed another grin as he turned to fully face Calandra. The gown was in place, wrapped firmly around her body, her lips thin and tight as she stared at him, hands by her sides and curled into fists. The coldness in her gaze would send most men running.

But not him. Not anymore. Not after the delights she had placed within his grasp last night as she'd wrapped those stunning legs around his waist and—

"Sorry, what?" he asked, dragging his mind back from his lurid fantasies.

"Thank you for…" She waved her hand in the air, then shook her head. "I hope you have a safe trip to New Orleans."

Panic flared in his stomach, unexpected and unwelcome. He never panicked when a woman left his bed. Usually he was the one doing the leaving. So why did it bother him that Calandra was practically running into the living room of the suite? Easier to deal with a woman who left on her own than one who took a single night as a sign of something more.

But Calandra leaving bothered him. Before he could examine his emotions, he gave in to instinct and jumped out of bed, grabbed a pair of sweatpants he'd tossed over a chair and followed her.

She had her hand on the door handle when he walked into the living room. Her eyes widened and focused on his chest and then snapped back up, her face red.

Ah. The ice queen wasn't nearly as impervious as she portrayed herself to be.

"What are you doing?" Her tone, on the other hand, could have frozen hell. "I said goodbye."

"It would be rude of me not to walk you back to your room."

Her lips tightened even further. Ever since Adrian had hired her three years ago, Alejandro had delighted in teasing her, trying to get a rise out of the woman who seemed to prefer business over pleasure.

Until last night. Last night, she had definitely preferred pleasure when she'd gasped his name as her hands had clutched his shoulders. He could still feel the heat of her fingertips on his skin.

"I don't have a room here."

Alejandro frowned. "Why not?"

"I'm staying with a friend in the city."

Jealousy slithered through his chest. "A friend?"

She didn't bat an eye at the sudden tension in his tone. "Yes."

"Anyone I know?"

"No."

It shouldn't bother him. They'd had one night together. One night was usually all he made time for. If her fleeing his hotel suite was any indication, Calandra wasn't interested in anything more, either.

So why was he jealous?

She opened the door and walked out. Alejandro

caught the door before she could close it and stepped out into the hall.

"Shouldn't you put on a shirt?" Calandra kept her gaze averted as she stalked down the hall to the elevator, the plush carpet masking the sound of her heels. An elderly couple walked past him, the woman's mouth dropping open as she took in his bare chest. The husband made a sound of disapproval and tugged his wife's hand, urging her along.

"I'm comfortable. Besides," he added with a grin as the elevator dinged and the doors whooshed open, "nothing you haven't seen before. Or kissed. Or nibbled—"

"I get it."

Before she could close the elevator doors in his face, he stepped in beside her and pressed the button for the first floor. The doors closed.

And suddenly they were alone once more in a very tight, very intimate space. He heard the sharp intake of her breath, felt the snap of electricity between them. He went hard in an instant, memories of their lovemaking rushing through his mind as his blood roared in his ears.

Mine, mine, mine.

He risked a glance down. Calandra stared straight ahead. She thrust her shoulders back, pressing her breasts against her neckline. That dark hair tumbled down her back, and he barely stopped himself from reaching out and tangling his fingers in the silky tresses.

The thought of her leaving the hotel room had filled him with a sense of urgency, almost a desperation to keep her in his sights. But now, as he took a step away from her and the temptation to press her up against the wall of the elevator and kiss those luscious lips, warning bells clanged.

Suddenly, he couldn't wait to be rid of her and the urges she inspired.

The elevator stopped and the doors opened, revealing the lobby. Grecian columns marched down the room, flanked by urns spilling over with deep pink blooms. A row of chandeliers hung from the ceiling. Soft instrumental music shut out most of the noise from Fifty-Third Street as taxis, buses and cars rushed by the floor-to-ceiling windows.

Calandra marched out of the elevator, heels clicking on the rosewood floor. Alejandro followed at a casual pace. As much as he wanted to return to his room, order breakfast in bed and catch a few more hours of sleep before his flight, he forced himself to do the right thing and at least see Calandra safely into a taxi.

The front desk attendant glanced up and did a double take as he passed, her eyes widening behind her enormous glasses.

"Um…sir—"

He winked at her. "I know, forgot my shirt. I'll make it right in a minute, I promise."

He quickened his pace as Calandra burst out the front doors and raised her arm. By the time he walked outside, she'd already hailed a cab and was reaching for the car door.

"Allow me."

Alejandro opened the door with a flourish and bowed. She tossed him a narrow-eyed glare as she climbed into the car.

"Thank you," she murmured stiffly.

"You're welcome."

She turned her head, probably to deliver a cutting remark, but whatever she was about to say was lost as their eyes met. The coldness disappeared once more, steel softening into misty gray that flared bright with desire, longing and…

He blinked. Something so sad it tugged at his heart.

"Calandra, I—"

She shook her head and reached for the door.

"Goodbye, Señor Cabrera."

The door slammed shut, and the taxi sped off. He watched it until it was swallowed up in the sea of New York traffic.

He glanced up at the legendary city's skyscrapers, despising the ache in his chest. The feeling that something wasn't quite right had been building for the past few months, a dissatisfaction with the endless parties and, if he dared to be honest with himself, a longing for something more. Something permanent. The two upcoming new ships that would be added to Cabrera Shipping's fleet had assuaged some of the emptiness. So had the tentative approval of the board to move forward on the *La Reina* project, despite his father's increasingly pointed comments about all the things that could go wrong. Not unexpected. He'd gotten used to Javier Cabrera's disapproval a long time ago.

The future was bright. So why did this longing for something more persist? And why had his night with Calandra tilted his world even farther off its axis?

He didn't know how long he stood there, staring at the spot where she'd disappeared, an uncomfortable ache tugging at his heart. But a sudden whoop, followed by a "Hey, sexy" from a bleary-eyed woman with smudged eyeliner hanging out the window of a passing cab, yanked him out of whatever nostalgic land he'd ventured to and back into reality.

One night. One night of mind-blowing sex. That's all it was, and that's all he wanted it to be.

With that final thought, he turned and walked back into the hotel. The clerk stood behind the desk, arms folded and eyes narrowed. Her black-and-gold name tag proclaimed her name to be Leia.

"Sir, we ask that all our guests wear a shirt, pants and shoes in the lobby."

He grinned and leaned against the counter. Instead of swooning or eyeballing his chest, her eyes tapered into slits.

Two women who'd resisted him in one morning. Maybe he was losing his touch.

He held up a hand in surrender. "I'm sorry. I wasn't paying attention. It won't happen again."

She stared at him for another long moment, then nodded toward the door.

"I hope your friend enjoyed her stay with us."

The smile disappeared from his face. "Yeah." Why did it bother him that Calandra had fled? He'd left plenty of beds without even a goodbye. He didn't care for being on the receiving end.

A flicker of compassion crossed Leia's face. "It could work out."

He returned Leia's gaze before smiling slightly. "Thanks. And I am sorry."

She pushed her glasses up the bridge of her nose and nodded briskly. "Yes, well…just don't do it again, Mr. Cabrera."

He backed away with his hands held up in surrender, shot her another thousand-watt smile that did nothing more than make her roll her eyes and headed for the elevator. The door swished open and a beautiful blonde woman rushed out, head down, hand clutched tightly around her suitcase. She glanced up. Recognition flared. He'd seen her dance with Adrian last night, seen the way his normally uptight brother had looked at her.

He started to say hello, to at least glean her name, but she dashed by so quickly he didn't even have a chance.

Oh, well. He had problems of his own. Like keeping his company moving forward and forgetting the woman who had run from his bed like the hounds of hell were nipping at her heels.

All while looking insanely sexy and deliciously rumpled.

Step one: cold shower. Step two: get dressed, grab breakfast. Step three: head to the airport. Step four: put Calandra Smythe and their incredible night together out of his mind.

CHAPTER TWO

Four months later

CALANDRA SURVEYED THE crowd gathered on the lawn of Adrian Cabrera's Paris home, her fingers curled around her champagne flute like it was a lifeline. People moved in a sea of summer colors, mint-green gowns and pale blue dress shirts, as they sipped on champagne and snacked on mushroom tartlets.

To think, the crème de la crème of European society considered this an intimate gathering. She'd been a part of this crowd when she worked for Adrian, not to mention the first thirteen years of her life.

But that was the past. A problem demanded her immediate attention. She would prefer to be home in North Carolina curled up in bed with a book and a cup of tea, but her conscience demanded that she address it.

A quick conversation. Just a couple minutes, and then you can leave.

Slowly, she eased the death grip on her glass before she broke it. He had no reason to be upset. She had a plan and would take care of everything, just like she always did. Besides, how many times, during their verbal sparring at various Cabrera Wine events, had he said he was a no-strings kind of guy? He eschewed commitment of any kind.

When he'd walked her down to that cab, she'd seen him in the rearview mirror standing on the sidewalk, gazing after her. And in that moment, a terrifying emotion had taken root—*want*. Not the burning, physical attraction she'd experienced that night, but a desire for the safety she'd experienced curled up in his arms.

She'd given herself a stern talking-to about all the reasons why such an emotion was dangerous. It implied commitment, something Alejandro clearly wanted no part of. Commitment she didn't want, either. Marriage had been crossed off her list long ago.

Even after she'd explained why she had no interest in getting him involved, her sister, Johanna, had encouraged her to reach out. After her younger sibling's relentless guilt tripping, she'd finally tried getting in touch. First by email, then by phone. Her emails went unanswered, her calls stonewalled by a terribly efficient secretary.

So she'd resorted to crashing an engagement party for the boss she'd walked out on over three months ago. She wouldn't have bothered if she hadn't been in London, she told herself, and the ticket from London to Paris had been manageable on her limited budget. Her final round of interviews for an event planner position with an elite European fashion house had included a round-trip plane ticket. An indicator, Johanna had excitedly said, that interview or not, the job was hers.

The interview that had gone south when they'd asked if they could contact Adrian Cabrera for a reference if they offered her the job. Her fourth interview in six weeks. Another reason why coming to this party was a good idea. Perhaps, along with sharing her important news with Alejandro, she could also somehow finagle a recommendation from Adrian. She might not have left on the best of terms, but she'd done damned good work for him in the time she'd given to Cabrera Wines.

She longed to sip the champagne in her hands, to feel the bubbles dance down her throat and soothe her galloping heartbeat. It had quickened into a fast-paced tempo when her plane had landed yesterday morning. It had kicked into a frantic pace this afternoon as she'd pulled on one of her last remaining evening gowns, the rest sold to give a feeble boost to her rapidly dwindling savings. And ever since she had boldly walked into the party like she belonged, her heart had pounded so ferociously she was amazed no one else could hear it.

"Beautiful, isn't it?"

Calandra reined in her runaway thoughts and schooled her features into a politely blank mask before turning to see who had interrupted her musings.

A tall brunette stood next to her, eyes fixed on the Eiffel Tower, standing tall and proud against the backdrop of a darkening sky.

"First time in Paris?"

As much as she loathed small talk, something about the young woman's waiflike innocence tugged at her. When she turned to look at Calandra, she bit back a gasp. The innocent wonder in the young woman's gaze was enhanced by her two differently colored eyes, one the palest shade of blue, the other a bright amber.

The young woman nodded eagerly. "Yes. I've lived in Spain since I was ten. I always dreamed of seeing Paris."

Protectiveness unexpectedly reared its head. Calandra kept her hands wrapped around her glass and resisted the urge to drag her away. Away from the glitter and shine that concealed far too many wolves in sheep's clothing.

"My name's Annistyn, but my friends call me Anna."

"Calandra."

"How do you know Adrian and Everleigh?"

"I used to work for Cabrera Wines."

Anna's eyes lit up. "I live at Casa de Cabrera in Granada. My uncle Diego is the butler."

Calandra smiled slightly. She had fond memories of the silver-haired steward of the Cabrera mansion.

"Oh."

Calandra followed Anna's gaze to where Adrian and his fiancée, Everleigh, stood on the terrace overlooking the lawn. Blood roared in her ears. Had they seen her? Would they call security and have her thrown out before she could accomplish her mission?

Breathe. Stay in control.

They weren't even looking in her direction. No, they only had eyes for each other. A handsome young man approached them, his smile flashing white against his dark brown beard. Adrian laughed and hugged him.

Calandra blinked. She could count on one hand the number of times she'd seen Adrian laugh.

"Um, excuse me."

Before Calandra could say another word, Anna turned and disappeared down a garden path. Calandra turned back in time to see Everleigh kiss the younger man on the cheek. Judging by the similarities in appearance, she was finally seeing Antonio Cabrera for the first time. The youngest brother had never attended Adrian's events, at least while she'd been working for Cabrera Wines.

Unlike Alejandro, who had attended almost every one and sought her out. He'd thrived on vexing her, tugging at the loose threads of her patience that only he seemed to be able to find. With everyone else she stayed calm, cool, unaffected.

With him, she turned into someone she didn't recognize. Someone who, for one wicked night, had thrilled at the touch of a hand on her face, a whisper in her ear, who now craved the closeness of sleeping next to someone and feeling their heartbeat beneath her fingertips.

A fool. He turned her into an irrational, dreamy-eyed fool.

She glanced around the party once more. No sign of him. She exhaled, long and slow, the tension melting from her shoulders. A soft breath in, followed by another long exhale.

She could do this.

One more glance over the crowds. No glimpse of the long, dark curling hair or deep blue eyes glinting with a lethal combination of seduction and humor.

Her eyes sought out Adrian and Everleigh once more. Conviction charged through her veins as she lifted her chin.

Before her resolve wavered, she set her untouched glass of champagne on a tray, pulled up the hem of her dress and marched across the lawn, keeping Adrian and Everleigh in her sights. As she advanced up the stairs, Adrian's head turned and he saw Calandra. Recognition widened his eyes, followed by a narrowing as his gaze turned stone-cold.

Should she have expected anything less? She'd abandoned her boss during his time of need, and had done so in a very unprofessional way. If Adrian knew the real reason she'd left, she had no doubt he would turn her life into a living hell.

One foot in front of the other. With each step her courage grew, propelling her forward as she reached the top of the stairs.

"*Buenos días*, Señor Cabrera."

Her voice came out firm, steady, a touch of friendliness in her tone. She held out her hand and kept it there, waiting.

Adrian stared at her for a long moment before finally shaking her hand. "It's been a while, Calandra. How are you?"

Everleigh elbowed her fiancé in the side even as she sneaked a curious glance at Calandra. "Be nice, Adrian."

"I am."

Everleigh rolled her eyes and, before Calandra could say anything, enveloped her in a hug.

Calandra froze for a moment before her brain kicked in. She tentatively patted Everleigh on the back. Everleigh released her, her face wreathed in a huge smile.

"I'm guessing you're Calandra Smythe? I've heard a lot about you."

"Nothing good, I'm sure."

Everleigh waved a hand. "I've only heard Adrian's side of the story. I'm sorry he's being discourteous. And at our engagement party, too."

Adrian's lips thinned. "Speaking of, I don't recall seeing you on the guest list."

"Adrian!" Everleigh exclaimed. "That's just rude."

"There's no need to apologize," Calandra said quickly. "I'm the one who should apologize. I came without an invitation. And I behaved very unprofessionally and left you in a bind." She looked directly at Adrian. "I'm sorry. I let a personal situation affect my work, and you bore the consequences."

Adrian returned her gaze with his trademark stare, the one that made men with years of experience quake in their boots. She didn't like talking, she didn't like apologizing and she definitely did not want to be around the Cabrera family any longer than she had to.

But she didn't back down.

At last, Adrian bowed his head briefly toward her. "Apology accepted."

Relief flooded through her. "Thank you."

Everleigh went up on her tiptoes and kissed his cheek. "I knew you had it in you."

Seeing the adoration in Adrian's eyes as he kissed his fiancée made Calandra's chest tighten. Her father's philandering and her mother's pining for the man who would never love her the way she loved him had ruined any girlhood dreams of Prince Charming. Love wasn't wedding bells and rosy baby cheeks. Love was crying until there were no tears left. A fairy tale with a monster lurking on the last page.

"Congratulations to you both. I'm very happy for you, Adrian."

She didn't believe in love or marriage, but that didn't mean she wished ill for anyone pursuing the elusive dream of true love. She meant her well wishes to the couple, every word. There were traces of the Adrian she had worked for, but he seemed happier, more relaxed.

Hopefully, unlike the early years of her parents' marriage that had turned from bliss to nightmare, his happiness would last.

"Thank you, Calandra." He snaked a possessive arm around his fiancée's waist and pulled her close. "But I can't help thinking that you didn't come to Paris just to wish us a happy engagement."

The perfect opening. She took a deep breath. First, recommendation. Second, where his brother was. She could do this.

"Hello, Calandra."

The world screeched to a halt as her hair stood on end, that sensual, deep voice sliding over her skin and touching the deepest parts of her illicit desires. Blood pounded in her veins so loudly the rest of the party noises faded around her. She turned, slowly, desperately trying to stay calm as her gaze locked onto a familiar pair of deep blue eyes.

Alejandro Cabrera. The father of her child.

CHAPTER THREE

THE CALANDRA SMYTHE standing before him was not the one he'd seen disappearing into the sea of New York traffic. That Calandra had been vulnerable, desire lingering in the uncertain gaze she'd shot him before running away. This Calandra was the one he remembered from her years at Cabrera Wines: dark, impervious, ice-cold as she stared at him with silver eyes so sharp they could cut a man to ribbons with a mere glance.

But he knew better now. He knew that beneath the ice ran a current of hot passion that had kept him awake for weeks after their tryst. Just the memory of making love to her, of her nails raking down his back as he'd slid in and out of her wet heat, sent raw hunger pulsing through him for the first time in four months.

Obsessiveness spread through his veins and rooted him to the spot. Even as he nodded to Adrian and kissed Everleigh on the cheek, he soaked in every detail of Calandra's appearance. The dark hair wrapped into a bun at the nape of her neck. The dash of deep burgundy on her lips. The swish of black satin that clung to her torso and flared out just below her breasts into a soft, loose skirt that fell in ripples to her ankles.

A surprisingly whimsical style on her. He never would have thought her the romantic type.

Just a month ago, he'd typed her name into Google, his finger hovering over the Enter key. He didn't know how long he'd sat there, contemplating what he would do if he actually found her, called her. Really, what was there to say? They'd had a one-night stand and, less than three weeks later, she'd quit his brother's company without notice and disappeared.

A sting to his pride. Nothing more. He'd never had a woman flee as if the devil were on her heels. Calandra's sudden departure and ensuing silence had been a novelty. That was the only reason he'd thought about her since.

At least that's what he'd told himself.

In the last few weeks, he'd barely thought of her at all. Javier's interferences had monopolized his thoughts day and night.

With the slightest shake of his head, he slipped into his playboy persona and flashed a smile in her direction.

"I'm surprised to see you here. And dressed in almost not black. What's the occasion?"

Everleigh sucked in a breath.

"Don't worry," Adrian said wryly. "They bicker like brother and sister."

Oh, no. Bickering like two people who couldn't stand that they were so attracted to each other, yes.

Most definitely not like brother and sister.

Unlike their previous encounters, though, Calandra did not take the bait. Her eyes darted to the side as she bit down on her lower lip. Her hand drifted to her stomach before she clenched her fingers into a fist.

Initially she'd seemed calm and collected. But now she seemed…nervous.

His eyes narrowed. He'd seen Calandra nervous exactly one time, and one time only—right after she'd kissed him senseless in an elevator in New York City.

Something was wrong.

She shot a stiff smile at Everleigh. "It's okay. I've gotten used to his teasing. It brings back memories of high school, actually. Same levels of maturity, too."

A grin tugged at his lips. Yes, the sex had been amazing, but even before they'd seen each other naked, he'd thoroughly enjoyed their verbal sparring. Calandra was the one woman who hadn't been afraid to stand up to him, to call him out or flat-out roll her eyes.

She was the only woman he'd ever felt truly comfortable around.

She turned those gray eyes on him, and his chest tightened. Yes, something was definitely wrong. Calandra kept herself aloof, always in control of any situation. He'd watched her navigate everything from drunk guests to a caterer who'd shown up thirty minutes before dinner was supposed to be served. She never batted an eye at the myriad things that had gone wrong in the years that she'd worked for Cabrera Wines. She'd simply adapted and overcome.

So what problem had caused this unrest in her, this nervous energy that practically sizzled across her alabaster skin? Adrian and Everleigh appeared unfazed. Could no one see the unease in her eyes, in the slight drumming of her fingers on the balcony railing?

"Alejandro, I need to speak with you."

Adrian's head whipped around, his eyes narrowing. Before Alejandro could open his mouth and come up with some witty retort, Everleigh, God bless her sweet soul, wound her arm through her fiancé's and tugged him toward the stairs.

"I think the fireworks are about to start, my love."

"But—"

"Off we go."

And just like that, they were alone. The seconds stretched out, each one longer than the last, as Calandra's gaze darted from the crowd gathered on the lawn to the marble staircase to the darkening Parisian sky.

Everywhere but him. Frustration tightened his jaw. She was the one who had sought him out, who had blazed her way into his brother's anniversary party to talk with him and now couldn't even look at him.

"What did you want to talk to me about?"

His direct question seemed to startle her out of her uncharacteristic state. Her lips parted as she sucked in a breath and started to speak…

Only for the boom of fireworks to cut off whatever she'd been about to say. Alejandro turned just as sparks burst above them, a shower of green and silver streaks that lit up the sky.

Below him, Adrian drew Everleigh into the circle of his arms, resting his chin on her golden head as she snuggled into his embrace.

A vise tightened around Alejandro's heart. The possibility of a long-term relationship, let alone marriage, was off the table. He'd sworn off long-term anything the day he'd walked into the library and discovered that his father wasn't an emotionally distant taskmaster with a fondness for rule following. No, he was much worse—a sanctimonious bastard who deserved to rot in hell for his selfishness.

It had nearly killed him to keep that secret all these years. But Madre was happy. He couldn't bear to shatter the illusion that Javier had somehow managed to maintain all these years. So he'd taken to punishing his father the one way he could—by engaging in the activities Javier loathed. The vices he indulged in had the added benefit of suspending the pain of rejection. Temporarily. Which was why he sought them out again and again.

He glanced at Calandra out of the corner of his eye. Her flight had added insult to injury, ripping off the bandages he'd been slapping over his wounds with reserved tables at the most exclusive clubs across Europe, casual sex and luxury cars.

But he'd also invested, scheduled the construction of two new ships to bring Cabrera's cargo freighters into the twenty-first century. Now, the first project that was truly his and his alone, *La Reina*, bordered on the brink of disaster, brought there by Javier's machinations. He wouldn't back down, though.

"Alejandro?" Calandra appeared next to him, a small V between her brows. He'd never pictured her as the emotional type. "Are you all right?"

"Yes. Got lost in my own thoughts. It's been an interesting couple of months."

A breathy laugh escaped her lips. "You have no idea."

He turned to see her face lit up by the constant stream of fireworks bursting overhead. Shades of blue, red and gold caressed her skin. His depressing thoughts faded away as he remembered just how good they'd been together, how tightly her body had wrapped around him as he'd moved inside her, the flare of emotion in her eyes when she'd looked up at him as if seeing him for the first time.

He'd always shied away from bringing emotions into sex. Hard to remain a bachelor when feelings got involved. But with her, the unexpected tenderness he'd experienced had added a heightened pleasure that had burned inside him long after she'd fled.

His groin tightened.

"Let's go inside where it's quieter. This sounds like a serious conversation."

She hesitated, then nodded. Triumph emboldened him as he reached out, grabbed her elbow and steered her toward the balcony doors that led into the library. He gestured for her to enter and closed the doors behind him. A quick tug and green velvet drapes fell over the glass, throwing the room into darkness, save for the dim light filtering in from the windows up above.

Something clicked. A lamp blinked on as Calandra looked around the room. Alejandro quelled his irritation. Light wasn't suitable for seduction. Although, he amended as the light shone through the fabric of her skirt and illuminated the curves of her legs, maybe it wasn't a bad thing.

Calandra circled the room, arms wrapped around her waist. Her eyes took in the books crowding the floor-to-ceiling shelves.

"Reminds me of the library from *Beauty and the Beast*."

"Singing teapots and a magical rose? Doesn't seem like your kind of movie."

A bitter smile twisted her lips. "Ice and snow and a beast with a cold heart. Seems just like me."

Normally he would have responded with a witty joke or some pithy comment about her remarkable resemblance to the ice sculptures that had often stood guard over the food at his brother's events. But the pain in her voice stopped him, as did the hurt that tightened her jaw as she pulled a book off the shelf.

"I beg to differ," he replied as he walked toward her. "You remind me of the candelabra that's always ordering everyone about."

She glanced at him over her shoulder, her prim expression somehow sexy. "I can't recall ever being on fire."

Oh, but I can. If she realized what she'd said, she gave no indication as she looked back down at the book in her hands. He walked toward her, each step upping his desire. His fingertips burned at the memory of how hot her bare skin had been beneath his touch. Excitement and lust heightened his senses as he stopped just a foot away.

"What did you want to talk about?" he whispered into her ear.

Her head snapped up and she turned, her mouth so close to his all he had to do was lean forward and claim her.

Her lips parted. He leaned in, ready to kiss her.

"Your child."

The words hung in the air. He drew back and stared down at her. He'd heard the words, knew they'd been spoken, but couldn't fully comprehend.

"My what?"

Her fingers came up and clenched the pendant around her neck so tight her knuckles turned white. "Your child, Alejandro. I'm pregnant."

CHAPTER FOUR

THE SECONDS DRAGGED on, each one growing longer as Alejandro stared at her.

Nothing. Not a flicker of emotion in those dark blue eyes. A blank visage, lips turned up slightly at the corners. The perfect poker face. A moment ago he'd been about to kiss her, and weakling that she was, she'd considered letting him, just to have one more taste before she dropped her bombshell.

Her brain had come to her rescue, and she'd forced out the words that would drive a wedge between them. Yet she hadn't expected this. Anger, shock, even a snide remark or a ribald joke. But of the myriad scenarios she'd planned for, complete and total silence was not one of them. Silence that stretched and filled the library with its oppressing presence, pushing against her until she was thrust back into the past and those terrible, awful mornings of endless quiet, save for the whisper of her mother's labored breathing.

Say something!

One last boom of fireworks reverberated outside. Another moment of even more oppressive silence. Then music struck up once more, sultrier, more seductive.

Just like that night. Try as she might, she couldn't

shake the memory of a darkened ballroom and a handsome man with his sleeves rolled up to his elbows, tan skin contrasting sharply with the white of his shirt.

The shirt she'd ripped off him less than an hour later in a passionate frenzy she'd never thought herself capable of.

Her lips thinned. Alejandro was dangerous. He brought her to the edge of control. Like now. Anyone else could have given her the silent treatment and she would have shrugged, turned and left.

But for him, she lingered. Waited. She hated it, yet she couldn't seem to walk away.

At last, he moved. He slid his hands into his pockets, broke eye contact and looked down at the balcony.

"Huh."

Blood pounded in her ears. She'd flown across an ocean, nearly two thousand dollars on plane tickets, a hotel room and a cab to sweet-talk her way into a party to tell the spoiled second son of a billionaire family she was pregnant with his child, and all she got was a damn *huh*!

She shouldn't have expected anything more. But she had.

In that moment, she hated Alejandro Cabrera. Hated him and his cavalier attitude, his lack of thought for anyone but himself. Common sense kept her from slapping him across the face. It would only be another display of emotions, a sign of weakness.

No matter how satisfying it would be.

Alejandro walked over to the balcony door, opened it and signaled to someone outside. Moments later, a waiter dressed in a silky black vest and bow tie appeared in the doorway, a silver tray with bubbling flutes of champagne perfectly balanced on his gloved hand. Alejandro plucked a glass from the tray and dismissed the waiter before he moved to a bank of windows. With a quick tug on a cord, the curtains fell back to reveal the sparkling lights of Paris on the horizon. The way he leaned against the windowsill, one trousered leg crossed casually over the other, glass in hand, looked like an ad selling thousand-dollar bottles of champagne.

"I'm not here for money. I'm taking care of everything." *Barely.* "But she—"

"Have you picked out names?"

Calandra blinked. A simple question, and yet how strange coming from his lips.

"We've picked out a few."

His head whipped around. She barely stopped herself from taking a step back at his darkening eyes.

"We?"

He uttered the word in a silky voice, but uncharacteristic anger lurked in his tone.

"My sister, Johanna." His shoulders relaxed. "She lives with me."

He looked back down at his drink. "So, if it's not about money, then what do you want?"

"To do the right thing. To let you know you have a child on the way."

His smile flashed once more, but this time it held an edge to it. She blinked, and it was gone.

"How quaint."

He took another long drink of his champagne and turned, eyes fixing on her face. She resisted the urge to squirm under his scrutiny.

"You flew all the way to Paris just to tell me?"

"I tried emailing. And calling."

He frowned. "I never received anything from you."

"If the secretary who refused to put my calls through also answers your emails, that explains it."

His lips twitched. "Yes, Laura is frighteningly efficient." His fingers tapped out a rhythm on his glass. "How much is all this going to cost you, anyway?"

"I have it handled."

No smile, no glint of teasing. Just a hard stare that made her want to squirm.

"Where do you work?"

"None of your concern." Her words whipped out, sharp and cold. She barely stopped herself from wincing. Why could she not keep her cool around this man?

He didn't even flinch.

"So," she continued, her voice calmer, "now that you know about the…the baby, I can keep you updated." Just saying *baby* made her feel possessive, protective. Strange, because she'd never imagined having children before. But ever since she'd seen the heartbeat pulsing across the monitor, she'd known she would do anything for the tiny human growing inside her, including keeping it safe.

Even from its own father.

"Updated?" Alejandro repeated.

"Photos, things like that. We can discuss events like birthdays and such later if you want to attend. But I know this is the exact opposite of your preferred lifestyle. And I have everything handled," she repeated.

There. She'd done it. She'd told him, set her boundaries. She suddenly felt lighter than she had in months. Now she could go home, close the door on this chapter of her life and move on with Johanna and her baby.

Despite the gravity of the situation, a tiny seed of happiness sprouted inside her. She been so focused on this confrontation, on telling Alejandro and getting it over with, that she'd barely thought about life with her child. But now that she had done the right thing, she was free. Free to buy books and booties and finally let Johanna drag her to the nearest store and start planning the nursery. A thought she would have turned up her nose at just a few months ago, but now…now she was going to be a mother. A mother who would never, ever let her child experience the pain she had.

She reached into her clutch and pulled out a card. Not having Alejandro involved in her and the baby's life was the best gift she could possibly give it.

"Here's my number and email if you have questions. Now that you know and know how to get ahold of me, I'll—"

He moved suddenly, crossing the floor and stopping within inches of her. She took a step back without thinking and bumped into a bookcase.

"You're not leaving, are you?"

"Yes. What else is there to say?"

His eyes narrowed. "You have a very clear idea of how this is going to work."

"Well, yes."

That smile reappeared, the one with the bite to it that revealed a glimpse of a darker, more serious Alejandro. She didn't like it.

"But you haven't asked me what I want."

"Given your history, it's obvious what you want."

He leaned in, balancing his hands on the bookcase and caging her between his arms. Her breath caught. He was so close she could see flecks of gold in the blue of his eyes, inhale the erotic aroma of pine that always clung to him.

"What do I want, Calandra?"

His voice came out husky and made heat pool between her thighs.

"To be free."

"I'll give you that. I used to want nothing more than freedom. To do what I want, with whom I wanted, when I wanted. But I've also had a tumultuous four months. And I've found that I want something else besides freedom. Something you've just handed me."

Warning pricked the back of her neck. "What?"

He stepped back, tucking his hands in his pockets and shooting her his thousand-watt grin. "I want to be a part of our child's life."

What? Her mouth dropped open, but no words came out. For once, she was speechless.

"Is that acceptable to you?"

"Um… I…"

He laughed, the rich sound breaking through the shock and drifting over her skin with disturbing sensuality.

"I need to mark this on my calendar. The first time you didn't have a snappy comeback."

"No, because I…" At last she found her voice. "You hate commitment."

The smile disappeared. The sight of him, lips tight, shoulders tense, jaw clenched, made her uneasy. What had happened to him? It wasn't just this moment, but something had been off all night, a darkness lurking behind the smile.

"Used to. People change, Calandra."

People did change. And other times, you thought

they'd changed, only to have them take your trust and rip it into tiny shreds.

"I don't think I'm comfortable with that."

"Because of my past?"

"I've seen enough pictures of what you've been up to the past four months. It's not your past that concerns me, but your present." Somehow her voice came out collected and cool. "My own father was like that. My childhood was a living hell. I won't have that for my child."

"Our child."

"*My* child," she repeated heatedly. "I'm going to be the one raising it, loving it, paying for it—"

"One million dollars."

She blinked. "What?"

"Or two million. Whatever you and the child need to live comfortably."

"You can't buy our child," she snapped.

"I'm not." Annoyance laced his voice. "I'm doing the right thing for *our* child, Calandra. The one I have a right to see."

Threads of fear tightened her chest into a fearful knot. She knew just how easily a man of Alejandro's resources and power could crush her, could use his wealth and lawyers to get shared or even sole custody. The reminder of who he was behind the charm only exacerbated the worry she'd been carrying since she'd decided to tell him about the baby.

Finally, she closed her eyes and let her head drop. Defeat sucked the energy from her limbs. Like it or not, it would be far easier to meet Alejandro halfway than fight him. Fighting could lead to a legal battle she couldn't even begin to afford.

"What do you want?"

The wooden floor creaked beneath his feet. A warm hand cupped her face. Startled, her eyes flew open and she looked up.

"I would like to be a part of our child's life." He held up a hand as she started to speak. "You have misgivings. Our relationship up until now has been... tempestuous."

Despite the gravity of the situation, amusement lightened her mood. "Fancy word for 'barely didn't kill each other.'"

His grin made her chest flutter. It had to be the excessive hormones pumping through her veins.

"You're the one who wanted to kill me. I just enjoyed teasing you. But we barely know each other. Not really."

She looked away. She didn't want to get to know him. Knowing someone meant time, emotions, investment. Things she wanted nothing to do with.

"What are you suggesting?"

"Stay tonight. Here. We'll talk in the morning."

"And if I refuse?"

Determination hardened his eyes and chased the pleasantness from his face. "If you refuse, then it becomes a legal problem."

His threat shocked her into silence. If this went to court, she would lose in a heartbeat. She couldn't even begin to compete with Alejandro's wealth or the lawyers he could buy. His menacing words solidified what she had suspected—beneath the smiles and gallant charm, he was just like her father. He toyed with people's emotions, manipulated them until he had what he wanted and then revealed his true self.

Her hand settled over her stomach as she lifted her chin. She'd play his game for now, maybe use the time to figure out why exactly he was so interested in becoming a father. Was there a business angle, like securing an heir—archaic as that notion seemed—or was it just male pride?

"Fine. We can talk tomorrow," she replied stiffly.

"Excellent."

"But I have a hotel room."

"Where are you staying?"

"Nearby."

He stepped closer. She stood firm. She despised him, hated him for having the power of wealth, for fooling her, for giving her a taste of what she thought had been true passion only to find out it was just a mirage.

Most of all, she hated that despite everything she'd discovered in the last five minutes, her body still responded to his dark, sensual masculinity.

"Stay here tonight."

Her spine straightened. Just because she was playing his game didn't mean she would take orders.

"No. Thank you."

His expression softened, but she kept her heart hard. She wouldn't be trapped in the vicious cycle her father had kept her mother in for years. Expensive trips, lavish gifts, a compliment designed to make the heart sing…until the next time he'd cheated. The next time he disappeared for a week and they'd had no idea if he was running wild in Europe or if he was lying in a ditch somewhere.

"It would be easier—"

"I said no." She spit out the words with such ferocity that she almost blinked in surprise.

Sadness darkened his eyes as he turned away. Her hand came up to…what? Stop him from leaving? Comfort him?

Don't fall for it.

He pulled back the curtain from the balcony doors and stepped outside, then looked back at her expectantly. He'd managed to turn this into a dismissal even though she was the one who was leaving.

Her defenses hardened. The last three years of conversations and bantering had revealed a keen mind and a sharp wit. Traits many people, including herself, had brushed aside because he seemed so utterly ridiculous. But then last year they'd talked more, delving into business, politics and travel. She'd learned that he was intelligent.

An intelligence she needed to be wary of as they moved into battle.

She walked across the library slowly, not giving him the satisfaction of hurrying to his side. As she started to move past him into the summer night, he caught her hand in his. Slowly, so achingly slowly, he brought her fingers up. She should pull away, should call him every insult she could think of. But no. No, she watched her fingers travel up to his mouth, bit down on her bottom lip as he pressed a kiss to her knuckles.

"Until tomorrow."

And with that he walked down the stairs to join the partygoers below. She watched his tall figure cut through the crowd with ease, pausing here and there to greet someone.

More than one female someone, she noticed.

It shouldn't bother her. It *didn't* bother her, she sternly told herself. The man had just threatened to take her to court over their child. He was a selfish, spoiled rich boy who, hopefully after she outlined all the responsibilities being a parent entailed, would run as far away from her as he could.

She would remain on guard. Rational. Logical.

Those thoughts did nothing to erase the burning sensation on the back of her hand where his lips had rested.

CHAPTER FIVE

THE NEXT MORNING, when Calandra rang the doorbell, a sweet-faced maid answered and ushered her into the grand hall of Adrian's Paris mansion, presided over by a crystal chandelier that probably cost as much as the mortgage on Aunt Norine's house. The maid murmured that Monsieur Cabrera would be out in a moment and disappeared. Moments later, the sound of raised male voices cut through the silence from one of the doorways off the hall.

"...don't know the first thing about being a father!"

Adrian's voice lashed out. Another voice responded, the faintest murmur, but it still sent a dangerous shiver down her spine.

Alejandro.

"How do you know she's telling the truth?"

Adrian's words cut deep. Shame rose in her throat, thick and bitter. The baby deserved so much better than her, a cold woman who'd succumbed to a moment of weakness with the last person she thought she would have slept with, much less taken as her first lover.

I'll do better, baby. I'll be better. For you.

Alejandro responded once more, his voice still so

low she couldn't make out his words. Silence ensued for several seconds. Then a door slammed.

"He's gone now."

She froze. Was he talking to her?

"I'm not going to bite, Calandra."

Another memory appeared with no warning, of his lips on her breasts, his teeth nibbling on her flesh as she'd arched up into his embrace.

She gritted her teeth. If she'd known sex would have caused this many moments of vulnerability, she never would have given up her virginity so easily. Or ever.

"Callie?"

"My name," she snapped as she advanced into the dining room, "is Calandra…"

Her voice trailed off as she stopped in the doorway.

The dining room, like the rest of the home, was elegant in the extreme. Black-and-white photographs of Paris, from the glass pyramid of the Louvre to the sweeping gardens of Versailles, decorated the cream-colored walls. Two-story windows marched along the far wall, sun streaming in to dance over the crystal chandelier that hung over a long, white table trimmed in gold.

On the left sat Alejandro, bare-chested, hair tousled and wearing a smirk that deepened the sexy dimple in his cheek. Clad only in burgundy lounge pants with a newspaper draped across his lap and his feet resting on the table, he raised his coffee mug to her in salute.

She tried to focus on those details, like the steam rising off the cup, and not on his chest.

His naked, tanned, muscular chest.

"Do you ever wear clothes?"

"They get in the way."

She rolled her eyes. Hopefully her outward irritation masked the unwelcome heat winding its way through her veins, leaving behind the desire to run her fingers over the carved muscles of his biceps.

"Your brother thinks I'm lying."

His smile grew, but this time his eyes crinkled at the corners. Funny, she'd never noticed that before. Almost like the smile he'd given her before was practiced, false, whereas this one was genuine.

"I missed that," he said before he took a sip of his coffee.

"What?"

"Your bluntness."

Not the most swoonworthy of compliments. So why did his words fill her with warmth?

Because you're just like your mother. You thought you were so strong all these years, but you're not. You're weak.

Her spine straightened as the heat in her veins turned to ice. The child growing inside her needed her to be strong. Needed her to stop her fantasizing and take charge of the situation.

"If you're hungry, the chef laid out quite the spread." He nodded toward a table on the far side of the room.

She nodded and walked over. She needed time to think, to regroup. Seeing him barely clothed had knocked her off balance. But as she put toast, sliced banana and a hard-boiled egg on her plate, her resolve strengthened. When she turned back toward the table, her walls were firmly back in place.

"How did you know I was here?"

He pointed to a mirror hanging on the far wall as she sat. "Not very sneaky."

"I wasn't trying to sneak." She took a bite of bread and let out a sigh. Lightly buttered, toasted to perfection.

A strangled sound came from across the table. But when she looked up, Alejandro was reading the paper in his lap.

"It sounded like Adrian thinks I'm trying to trap you."

Alejandro shrugged. "Doesn't really matter what he thinks. He's in big brother mode. Wants to make sure I don't make a mistake."

"Like marrying me?"

He let out a bark of laughter as he looked up. "I think we both know that would never happen."

Even though she had absolutely no desire to be shackled to him, or anyone for that matter, his emphatic statement still hurt.

"You do. I do. But your brother doesn't."

Years of suppressing her emotions helped her stay calm as she continued to eat her breakfast under his watchful gaze. But finally, after she'd taken another bite of toast and eaten half the banana, she looked up at him in irritation.

"It's rude to watch someone eat."

"Shouldn't you be eating more?"

Her fingers tightened around her fork. "On the list of things you can't tell me what to do, how much I eat is number two."

One eyebrow arched as his lips quirked. "And what's the first?"

"How to raise my child."

His feet dropped down as he spun in his chair, sitting up straight and leaning forward over the table. It should have looked comical, a shirtless man sitting amid the backdrop of so much luxury.

But the look on his face was anything but funny. Eyes narrowed and crackling with intensity, lips thinned, jaw tight. In that moment, he looked more like his brother than she'd ever seen him.

Except this was…*more*. She and Adrian had shared a similar disposition. When they took charge, they grew cold. Their command partially came from their ability to show as little emotion as possible.

Alejandro, on the other hand, channeled his usual charm and energy into a threatening force that threw her off balance.

"*Our* child."

His voice vibrated with suppressed anger.

"I acknowledge your anatomical contribution. And while I had not expected your interest in being a parent—"

"How could I not be interested?" he bit out.

"I don't have enough fingers and toes to count the times you told me and anyone within earshot that jumping into a shark-infested pool would be more preferable than marriage."

"Marriage, yes. Fatherhood, no."

Her confusion only heightened her own anger.

"How could you possibly expect me to separate those two? Oh, the man who sleeps with at least one new supermodel every week also wants to burp a baby and change diapers. A logical conclusion. How could I have missed it?"

Some of his anger faded as he leaned back in his chair and rubbed the bridge of his nose. "Why do you always have to be so cold?"

He was excelling at hurtful comments this morning. She wanted to respond truthfully, to snap out that she didn't like being cold. The world had made her this way.

Cold wasn't by choice. Cold was by necessity.

"If you'd leave me alone, you wouldn't be subjected to my company."

He sighed. "This is not how I wanted this conversation to go." He nodded toward her plate. "I'm not trying to control you, Calandra. I've never been around a pregnant woman before, much less one who's carrying *my* child."

Ignoring his emphasis on *my*, she focused on her water glass. "Impressive given your history."

"You're the first I've been irresponsible with." He grimaced. "I had condoms in my damn pocket. But I wanted you so much I just…forgot."

Damn her traitorous heart and the little jump it gave upon hearing those words.

"I see."

"I just want to make sure you're getting everything you need, including nutrients. I've heard the phrase *eating for two*." He nodded at her plate. "And that's barely enough to feed a bird."

She inhaled deeply. Condescending as his voice was, her mind pointed out that, surprisingly, he was just trying to help.

"I appreciate your concern. I wish I could eat more. I'm experiencing horrible nausea. Small meals are best right now."

He nodded, then glanced around the room. "What do you say we reconvene in the main hallway in ten minutes? I find walking and talking helps me relax."

"Walk to where?"

He smiled, his jovial nature restored. "It's a surprise."

She groaned. "Alejandro, I'm really not—"

"Please."

And just like that, he cut through her resolve, wielding sincerity like a sword. His use of a simple word laid waste to her armor like no sensual assault could.

"Fine."

He stood. She kept her eyes on his face.

"Ten minutes."

And with those parting words he scooped up his coffee and his newspaper and walked out of the dining room without a backward glance. Once his footsteps faded, she sank back into her chair and hung her head.

Years. For years she'd been impervious to men, to their looks, their attempts at seduction, their harshness when they didn't get their way. Anytime she'd entertained even the slightest thought of allowing one into her life, all she'd had to do was summon an image of her mother as she'd last seen her, paled by death and lying in a casket, and it had kept her armor in place.

She sighed. The doctor had told her it would be another few weeks at least before the baby would move. Aside from the nausea, most days it didn't seem real, that a child was growing inside her. But when she stopped and thought about it, really thought about it, she was overcome with a love so fierce it stole her breath away.

The first time she'd experienced that rush of emotion, she almost cried. Deep down, she realized, she'd sometimes wondered if she was truly good at suppressing her emotions or if she just couldn't feel them. She loved Aunt Norine and Johanna, but she'd never experienced emotions the way others had described them. The highs, the lows and everything in between.

Until Alejandro. And then their child. With Alejandro, it was dangerous. But with her child…yes, she could love her child with all her heart.

No one, not even Alejandro, with his fortune and power, would take her away from her baby. She'd make sure of it.

CHAPTER SIX

ALEJANDRO GLANCED AT Calandra out of the corner of his eye as they walked up the stairs of the Eiffel Tower. She moved with purpose, her gaze evaluating her surroundings with cool indifference, as if she wasn't walking up one of the most iconic monuments in the world. He'd offered the elevator; weren't pregnant women supposed to rest as much as possible? But she'd dismissed that idea with a shake of her head and started for the stairs before he had even finished paying for the tickets.

A gaggle of giggling young women hurried past them, their excited voices labeling them as American. One, a pert brunette with painted red lips and a deep V-cut shirt, flashed him a sexy smile and brazenly raked him from head to toe with her green eyes.

An invitation he normally would have leaped on in a heartbeat. He smiled slightly and shook his head. The girl shrugged and continued on with her friends.

It wasn't just that the mother of his child was by his side. In the past four months, he'd had almost zero interest in other women. He'd only been on one date— dinner in London with a popular actress. When he accompanied her back to her hotel, walked her to her door and she'd kissed him, he'd experienced…nothing.

He'd made an excuse. She'd flown into a rage, thrown a barrage of creative insults at his manhood and slammed the door in his face.

Production delays in the construction of Cabrera Shipping's latest freighter had consumed much of his time the first four weeks after New York. Concerned clients, worried stakeholders and an increasingly hostile board had led to late-night conference calls, plane trips around the world and endless pots of coffee. Toss in his mother's car accident, his older brother nearly drowning himself in alcohol and then Alejandro assisting Adrian in locking his future fiancée out on a balcony to propose to her, and he'd been downright swamped.

And the last three months...preparing how best to respond to his father's interference and threats had occupied the majority of his waking hours. It never mattered how many times Alejandro met the bar Javier had set, there was always room for him to raise it further still.

This little jaunt into Paris was a welcome break from the crisis mode he'd been operating in since Javier had set out to ruin his middle son. Serious discussion looming in the near future aside, he took the time to enjoy the warm sunshine on his skin, the sight of Paris laid out in all her historic splendor and the classic beauty of the woman at his side. Dressed in her customary black, a pencil skirt and loose-fitting silk shirt, hair coiled into a bun at the nape of her neck, she looked every inch the modern French woman. Elegant, sophisticated, untouchable.

He'd expected more of a reaction when she'd entered the dining room this morning. A flustered mumbling, an openmouthed stare. Her ice-cold response had simultaneously flummoxed him and flamed the banked coals of desire that had been smoldering inside his chest ever since he'd seen her on the balcony last night.

Never had he had to fight so hard to retain a woman's interest. It had always been that way with Calandra—perhaps it was why he'd sought her out over and over again at Adrian's events. She'd been an anomaly, the woman who resisted his charms. Not only had it been fun to see how far he could push the boundaries, but it had been refreshing. Most women fawned over his wealth, his flashy cars, his familial connection to the internationally recognized Cabrera name.

Not Calandra. When she'd simply rolled her eyes at him and gotten breakfast in response to his half-dressed state, it had taken every ounce of self-control not to close the doors to the dining room, drape her across the table and kiss her senseless until she moaned his name.

His eyes dropped from her pert nose and nude lipstick to her belly. Possession reared its head. No matter what sins he'd committed, he would never abandon his own flesh and blood. His child would know their father, would know they were wanted.

"Stunning, isn't it?" he asked, nodding in the direction of the grassy lawns of the Champ-de-Mars and, in the distance, the Corinthian architecture of the École Militaire school complex.

"Mmm-hmm."

She'd barely said "boo" when he'd escorted her out the front door to his Jaguar convertible. She hadn't batted an eye when they'd pulled up in front of the Tower and received exclusive valet service. All the tricks that normally worked on every other woman he'd met didn't faze her.

Uncertainty tugged at him. If he couldn't wow her with his wealth, with all the resources, gifts and support he could bestow upon their child, then what would work?

They reached the second floor. Calandra wandered to the edge of the observation deck and leaned against the railing. He pointed out the Louvre, the Champs-Élysées, lined with some of the most luxurious shops in the world, and the Arc de Triomphe.

She blinked in response.

"I've never met anyone more unimpressed by life," he said with a shake of his head as he leaned against the railing.

Out of the corner of his eye, he caught the barest flinch in her shoulders. Had he imagined it? A quick glance revealed nothing in the stoniness of her expression.

Yet he'd noticed the same thing this morning when he'd told her point-blank he would not be offering marriage. A nagging feeling that he'd hurt her.

Unfathomable, given her stalwart personality.

But she's not impervious.

He'd seen another side of her. A much more emotional and passionate side.

"Just because I don't share the story of my life with you doesn't mean I'm not impressed."

He turned and faced her. "Then tell me."

She frowned. "Tell you what?"

"What you're thinking."

"I don't see how that's relevant to the discussion we need to have."

The more she resisted, the more he wanted to know. It hit him that, despite having been acquainted with her for the past three years, he really didn't know anything about her. Other than that she had worked for Cabrera Wines, had a sister named Johanna and, until four months ago, she'd been a virgin.

"Humor me. Answer one question and then I'll devote myself to an entire five minutes of serious discussion. Ten," he conceded as she opened her mouth to object. "Ten whole minutes."

"Probably ten minutes longer than you've ever gone," she grumbled.

He started to correct her, to tell her about the hours he'd spent poring over numbers and reports with his chief financial officer or the seven board members he'd taken out to individual lunches, spending anywhere from an hour to three explaining why Cabrera Shipping should remain in his hands.

But he stopped. That part of his life, the reality that took place behind the media's coverage of his supposedly glamorous existence, was private. Calandra had already shown herself to be difficult to impress on multiple occasions. The thought of sharing that little bit of himself, the one piece of his life he took pride in, only to be faced with her judgmental silence, was not something his pride cared to experience. God knew he'd faced enough indifference from Javier to last a lifetime. Setting himself up for the same disappointment with the woman who was carrying his child was not an option.

Coward, the little devil on his shoulder whispered.

Yep, he mentally replied.

"Well?" he asked, his voice light and not showing

an ounce of his inner turmoil. "Ten minutes for your thoughts?"

She looked out again, her gray eyes roving over the rooftops of Paris.

"I was thinking…" She paused. Her chest rose and fell. He noticed the swell of her breasts—how could he not—but also the look of resolve on her pale face.

Again, that little flicker that he was missing something. There was so much he didn't know about her.

"I was thinking how good it will be to bring my… our," she amended with a glare in his direction, "our child to the top of the Tower one day."

Her words surprised him. She didn't strike him as the type to daydream or think about the future, unless it involved the seating charts she'd laid out oh so meticulously for Adrian's events.

"That sounds nice."

"I've met my part of the bargain." She glanced at the silver watch clasped around her wrist. "Ten minutes starts now."

Right back to business.

"I want to be involved in our…" His voice trailed off. "Are we having a boy or a girl?"

"I don't know."

He frowned. "Aren't they supposed to be able to tell by now?"

"I want to be surprised."

Another unexpected revelation. "But you plan everything. You counted how many roses were in each vase at that party in Switzerland. All fifty vases."

"And now I want to be surprised," she retorted.

He held up his hands in surrender. "I'm not opposed."

Silence and that frigid stare. He sighed. This was not going well at all.

"Calandra, as I stated before, I have no interest in taking the baby away from you. I don't know the first thing about kids. And I have no desire to part a child from a parent who obviously loves it so much already."

Her eyes softened. The effect was almost jaw-dropping. Her face relaxed, her mouth going from its customary strict line to tilting up at the corners. Instead of rigid and powerful, she appeared...approachable. Feminine.

Desirable.

"Thank you, Alejandro."

The words punched him in the gut. Her voice came out husky as her shoulders relaxed and she tucked a stray wisp of hair behind her ear.

"You're welcome," he responded dryly in an attempt to mask the effect she had on him. He glanced down at his watch. "I believe we ate through nearly three minutes with that little drama, so let's cut to the chase—I have two proposals for you."

Her guard immediately came back up. "Oh?"

Two proposals he'd stayed up until well past midnight contemplating. "Yes. My first—I will be involved in our child's life."

"Define involved."

"I want to visit. Regularly. As in," he continued as she opened her mouth, no doubt to ask for a definition, "a minimum of one week a month. Most likely two."

A frown crossed her face. Irritation tightened his muscles as his lust ebbed. Did she truly think so little of him that she could barely stand the thought of him being around their child?

"I can't just fly to France or Spain or wherever it is you jet off to for your parties."

"First, I have my own jet. I'll fly to you. I won't be exposing a child to parties, either."

He'd hoped she would refute his last statement, that she didn't think him that stupid. Her silence gave him his answer. He should be used to rejection and low expectations by now. Why did hers feel like someone had just carved his heart from his chest?

"Second," he continued, "an investigator friend of mine informed me you don't have a job."

Two bright red spots appeared in her cheeks. "You had no right to pry into my private life."

"I had every right." He kept his tone friendly but his voice firm. "You know so much about me. Fair is fair. Which brings me to my second proposal."

The V between her eyebrows deepened. "You're not giving me money."

"I am giving you money, but for the child."

"No."

"There's no room for disagreement on the money. I have more than I know what to do with. I'm not going to let our child grow up without the things they deserve—a good education, a nice home, security."

"I can provide all that."

"Without a job?" He knew the remark was harsh, but she had to understand, had to see the reality of her situation.

Her shoulders dropped. Just a fraction, but enough that guilt fizzled on the edge of his conscience. She turned to look out over Paris, her face averted.

"Your second proposal?"

Her voice was so quiet he instantly regretted his severe remark. Calandra was a fighter. She stood up to anyone and everyone, including him. To see her withdraw into herself was disheartening.

Before he could reply, a swarm of tourists disembarked from an elevator. A cacophony of languages swirled around them. Mothers grabbed onto errant children as excited couples, faces bright with awe and romance, grasped hands and rushed to the railing. One overly eager young man knocked into Calandra, and she stumbled. Alejandro moved fast, catching her in his arms and pulling her tight against his chest.

"Sorry, mate, I..." The young man's voice trailed off as he took in the cold fury in Alejandro's eyes. "S-sorry." He swallowed hard, grabbed his wide-eyed girlfriend and steered her away.

Slowly, the thundering of his heart abated. There were protections all over the Tower to keep the millions of tourists who visited it every year safe. But for one horrific moment Alejandro had seen Calandra pitch to the side, had envisioned her toppling over the railing to the pavement below.

His arms tightened around her.

"I can't breathe, Alejandro."

He almost missed it, the faint breathiness beneath the frigid tone. But when he looked down and saw her eyes burning like molten silver, assessed the color blooming in her normally pale cheeks, he knew that she felt it, too. Not just the desire but the magnetic pull that had drawn them together night after night for the past three years.

A satisfied smile spread across his face. Perhaps it wouldn't be so hard to convince her.

"Breathing is overrated."

She pushed him back. "I know a few billion people who would disagree with you." She smoothed the folds of her skirt as she turned back to the railing. Once again in control.

But not always. He had an effect on her. He wouldn't hesitate to use their chemistry to get what he wanted.

"I believe you had a second proposal for me."

He leaned on the railing and looked out over Paris. "Yes. I'd like to hire you as an event planner."

CHAPTER SEVEN

CALANDRA KEPT HER gaze focused on the scorched yet still proud towers of Notre Dame, standing resolute against the blue morning sky, as she processed Alejandro's words.

The first emotion to reveal itself in the tangled mess inside her chest: anger. Anger that he was only proposing this as a way of giving her money because he knew she wouldn't just accept a check.

Embarrassment was next, that hot, uncomfortable emotion that burned her cheeks. Before her epic fall from grace, she'd courted offers every year from industries around the world wanting to steal her away from Cabrera Wines. But she'd liked her job.

A job she'd thrown away. A blood test her doctor had ordered after she reported trouble sleeping had revealed her pregnancy. Hours later, Alejandro's name had jumped out at her on the proposed guest list for the party celebrating the joining of Cabrera Wines with Fox Vineyards. Images had cascaded through her mind, ranging from her blurting out her secret in the middle of the party to rushing to the nearest trash can with morning sickness as he paraded around the room with an actress or model or heiress, whatever flavor of the week he was indulging in.

Uncertainty and panic had driven her to do something impulsive—she'd quit. Better that than make a fool of herself. Her job hadn't been worth her pride, her self-respect. A week later, those pictures of Alejandro walking into a hotel in London with a famous actress had confirmed that she'd made the right decision.

Until a few weeks after that when she started receiving rejections and had faced the reality that, rather than make a smart decision, she'd once again done something uncharacteristic—she'd made a huge decision based on emotion, not practicality. She'd given up a job she enjoyed and a sizable paycheck that allowed her to pay for Johanna's nursing school as well as the rest of Aunt Norine's mortgage on her beachside cottage, on the possibility that she might see her one and only former lover.

A paycheck that had fueled a lovely savings account that was dwindling under the constant onslaught of bills and expenses.

Which brought her to her third and final emotion: hope. Hope that maybe this job, whatever it was, would not only provide her with a financial foundation before the baby was born, but might lead to her hearing *You're hired* instead of the copy-and-paste *Thanks for your time, but we've decided to go with another candidate* email she'd received too many of lately.

Her pride didn't like it. Actually, her pride hated it. Accepting any type of help made her skin prickle.

But it wasn't just about her anymore. Johanna, bless her, had taken on a part-time job at a nearby hospital and secured two scholarships that would see her through to graduation.

"Something I should have been doing all along," she'd chirped cheerfully when she'd shared the scholarship letter with Calandra. "Don't worry about me, sis." She'd rubbed Calandra's belly excitedly. "It's my turn to take care of you."

And that's what Calandra needed to focus on. Much as she preferred to do this alone, and as much as she didn't want to be around the man who put her into such a state of confusion, the baby was now the most important thing in her life. If that meant making some sacrifices, like accepting a little help from the devil himself, then so be it.

"Doing what?" she finally asked.

"Overseeing final preparations for a party."

She turned to look at him, then wished she hadn't. When she looked out over the buildings of Paris, she could admire the history, the architecture, map out the arrondissements and neighborhoods in her head if she needed something to focus on.

But when she looked at Alejandro, dressed to the nines in chestnut-brown shoes, tan slacks that clung to his muscular legs and a sky-blue shirt molded to his tall, burly frame, all rational thought fled. She envied the relaxation she'd spied on his face as they walked to the Tower. She'd been both tempted and terrified of the passion in his eyes when he'd held her close. It made her remember what it was like to have a man look at her with desire. With passion. To hold her like she was the most treasured thing he'd ever encountered.

Dangerous. Men like him were so dangerous. Her father had been like that, flashing his winning smile and showering her mother with compliments that would make any woman swoon...or he had until he'd turned his attentions elsewhere.

His eyes pinned her in place. A smile lurked about his lips, but now she knew better. After seeing how quickly he'd flipped this morning, taking charge of a situation and letting his facade slip to reveal the strength that ran beneath the surface, she kept her guard up. She'd always treated him like a puppy— silly, at times humorous and more often annoying.

Now she wondered how much of that was Alejandro and how much of it was a mask.

"I don't see cargo ships hosting the kind of parties I usually plan."

"I'm diversifying."

"To what?"

He joined her at the railing. A summer breeze teased his dark curls.

"We're in the process of completing construction on two new ships. Two more will join them over the next three years. Instead of scrapping one of the ships being replaced, I'm having it retrofitted into a floating hotel off the coast of Marseille."

Admiration rose in her chest. "An interesting concept."

He smiled. When he smiled like that, a real smile where his eyes crinkled at the corners and warmth brightened those dark blue depths, he was even more frustratingly handsome.

"I wish I could take credit for it. The Cunard Line did something similar with the *Queen Mary*. The ship we're retiring, *La Reina*, is in good condition. She's just old. Once a ship hits the thirty-year mark, clients and stakeholders get nervous."

The change in tone caught her attention, the serious, businesslike tone he'd occasionally let slip into their past conversations.

"Still, it must cost a lot to remake a cargo ship into a hotel."

"Yes and no. We're not doing the whole ship. Just the upper portions where guests will be staying and eating. The lower portion will be left as is."

Pride ran deep in his voice. His eyes usually glimmered with amusement or teasing, but it was excitement that lit them now. It lit a similar fire in her, all the possibility that *La Reina* offered. Crafting events from scratch and seeing her ideas come to life had been her favorite part of working for Cabrera Wines. "You could offer tours. Make use of the space."

His smile deepened. She fought the pleasant sensation that spread through her veins upon realizing that his smile was directed entirely at her.

"This is why I'd like to hire you. The board must approve my proposal. At the end of every fiscal year, we have a final meeting, vote on any major issues and then celebrate with a small party at my villa in Marseille. This year, a week from now, I'm hosting it on *La Reina*."

"So where do I fit into this?"

His face darkened as his eyes hardened. "My father is the majority stakeholder of Cabrera Shipping. He thinks I'm throwing money away on this idea. If the board votes against my proposal, let's just say my life will look very different."

She wanted to ask how, but his expression offered zero room for inquiries.

"I'm still not sure why you need me."

"One of the things that will make *La Reina* a success is if I give a glimpse into the luxury experience we'll offer. You specialize in such events. Help me sway them."

Her thoughts turned to the young man she'd seen on the balcony with Adrian and Everleigh the night before. "What about Antonio? He already runs successful resorts."

"He's helped me with the renovations, suite designs, that sort of thing. But he's busy with his own upcoming launch in Italy. And you," he said with a seductive smile, "have all the experience I need."

"Planning a party of that magnitude will take more than a week."

"Most of it has already been planned. But I need someone to bring all the pieces together, to supervise. Still a lot, which is why I'm prepared to pay you half a million dollars."

Her hands tightened on the railing.

"That's too much."

"No, it's not." He held up a hand as she started to object. "Whatever plans you put together have the potential to make my company, and therefore me, a lot of money."

"What if the board votes no?"

"They'll vote yes."

She envied his assurance, the complete and total confidence she'd had before she'd had sex. Was sex always so complicated?

"Two bonuses from this arrangement," he continued, oblivious to her questioning herself. "One—once completed, you'll have my personal reference that will secure you any job you want. And two, we get to know each other better so you're comfortable with me being involved as a father and we avoid the nasty legal battles."

Oh, it was a neat solution, all tied up with a pretty bow. Never mind it scared the hell out of her—a week alone with a man she could barely control herself around.

"I'll also help beyond the job. Financially."

She pinched the bridge of her nose. "Alejandro, you're already offering an outrageous salary—"

He grasped her hand and gave it a gentle but firm squeeze. "That part is nonnegotiable, Calandra."

She stalled for a moment, trying to think of something, anything else that might change his mind.

Nothing. Finally, grudgingly, she murmured, "All right."

The lock slammed on the door to the private hell she'd just created for herself. She'd spent her whole life avoiding becoming trapped by her circumstances the way her mother had. Wooed by a Swiss millionaire on a spring break trip in college and whisked from her modest home in the Carolinas to a mansion tucked between the Alps and Lake Geneva, her mother had been helpless when the dream had turned into a nightmare.

And now here she was, accepting a job offer, money, allowing herself to become a kept woman.

You're not your mother. Much as she'd loved her mom, what Lila Smythe lacked in strength and determination, Calandra had more than made up for over the years. Yes, she had to hand over a little bit of power now. But she would prevail.

"Scared, Calandra?"

His voice, so deep and yet so silky, so dangerous, wrapped around her, tantalizing, tempting, seducing.

She didn't immediately answer, because yes, she was scared, terrified even, that after only one night together he still stirred such longing in her. Time and experience had taught her that men like Alejandro were fun, until they weren't. Her child would grow up without the pain that had been her constant companions through childhood.

Which meant keeping men like Alejandro at arm's length.

Or an ocean's length, she thought as Alejandro took another step, the heat from his body kissing her skin.

What had she just done?

He leaned in. She stayed still, hand clutched around the railing of the Eiffel Tower like it was the only thing keeping her tethered to reason. She would not back down, would not succumb.

"Don't be scared." His smile deepened. "What's the worst that could happen?"

CHAPTER EIGHT

CALANDRA STRODE TOWARD the double doors of her boutique bed-and-breakfast. Beyond the glass and down the boulevard, the stone walls and elegant pillars of the entrance to the Louvre stood tall and proud.

Museums and tourist spots, from the Statue of Liberty in New York to the Eiffel Tower, had failed to pique her interest in the past. They were notable only in that others liked them, dreamed of them, crafted entire trips around seeing a monument. She'd worked plenty of icons into her events because the guests appreciated them—it had been good business, even if she'd failed to see the allure.

Yet when she stood on the deck of the Eiffel Tower yesterday, she'd meant what she had said to Alejandro. Some might say the magic of Paris had worked its way into her blood. Or perhaps she was just embracing the prospect of motherhood more as her waistline slowly but steadily expanded.

Whatever the reason, the thought of seeing her child squeal in delight as they saw Paris laid out before them filled her with a maternal warmth.

That she'd briefly entertained an image of Alejandro standing next to her, one hand intimately entwined with hers and the other on their child's shoulder, had irritated her.

Weak. Foolish.

She steeled her spine as her heels clicked on the wood floors. One week. One week to do a job that might reopen all the doors that had been slammed shut because of her brief but disastrous foray into the world of emotions.

One week to let Alejandro live out whatever fantasy he'd concocted of being involved. At the first sign of morning sickness or a reminder of how little sleep new parents achieved, he'd be gone.

The possibility that he would stick around frightened her in more ways than one.

She pushed open the door and stepped into the warm French sunshine, a bag hanging from her shoulder and a suitcase in hand. A couple stops on the Metro and she'd be at the station in plenty of time to catch her train to Marseille. Unexpected anticipation lent a barely discernible bounce to her step. Even without a job keeping her tied to a rigorous schedule, she'd spent her weeks editing her résumé, following up on job leads and staying busy. As always.

An uninterrupted train ride through the French countryside sounded like heaven.

"Mademoiselle Smythe?"

Calandra's head snapped up. A young man stood in front of her, dressed in a dark gray suit with a navy tie. Almost as young as Johanna, but with a much more serious air. A sleek black limo stood behind him, windows tinted so dark she couldn't see the interior.

"Who are you?"

The man bowed his head. "Your chauffeur."

"I didn't order a car."

"Monsieur Cabrera did, mademoiselle, with his compliments."

Her fingers tightened on the phone. Suspicion slithered up her spine as she barely bit back the retort that rose in her throat.

"Did he now?"

If the man sensed the danger lurking in her tone, he didn't reveal it.

"*Oui*, mademoiselle. I'm to take you to your destination before you continue to Marseille."

Hard to be angry at a thoughtful gesture even though her instincts were screaming at her to be cautious. Warily, she allowed the chauffeur to put her suitcase in the trunk and open the door. Black leather and cool air welcomed her into the luxurious interior.

The chauffeur hurried around and pulled away from the curb before she could change her mind. They passed the glass pyramid outside the Louvre, the sparkling waters of the Seine and the vivid green storefront of the legendary Shakespeare & Company, the sidewalk outside the shop crowded with shelves of books and tourists.

Just as she started to relax and enjoy the sights, her phone pinged. She pulled it out of her pocket and frowned as she read the message.

"'Your train ticket has been refunded'?" she read aloud. She looked up just in time to see the limo pass by the bridge that would have led to the train station.

Realization hit first, followed by a swift rush of anger so intense she barely stopped herself from cursing out loud. So much for Alejandro letting her make her own decisions. Did he think he could arrange everything to his liking?

By the time the limo pulled into a private airfield thirty minutes later, she had reined in her temper to a manageable level. The limo drove straight onto the tarmac and stopped next to a jet with the letter *C* emblazoned on the side in scarlet. Alejandro stood at the bottom of the stairs, eyes hidden behind his sunglasses, dark hair falling about his chiseled face. He looked like he'd just come from a magazine cover shoot—V-neck navy shirt stretched across his muscular chest, blue jeans hanging casually from his tapered waist. The grin he aimed at the window of the limo was playful. But beneath the casual smirk she now saw the edge, the determination in the firmness of his lips.

She'd underestimated Alejandro. Again. But, she reminded herself, each event like this gave her more insight into what she was fighting. It was a learning experience, not a failure.

"Buenos días, sol."

She arched a brow as she drew nearer, hardening her heart with every click of her heels. "Sunshine?"

"You brighten up my day by accepting my invitation."

"Invitation?" She returned his smile with a frigid one of her own. One that clearly let him know she would not be bought off nor controlled. "You and I have different definitions of invitation. *Threat* would be more accurate."

He stepped closer and whipped off his sunglasses. The intensity in his dark blue gaze almost made her step back. Almost. She stood straighter, one arm instinctively crossing over her waist.

Alejandro's gaze dropped down to her belly, and he frowned.

"Do you truly think I would harm you? Harm our child?"

"*My* child. And no, not physically," she admitted at the flash of what almost looked like hurt in his eyes. "But I don't appreciate you rearranging my schedule or canceling my train tickets. That's a violation of my privacy."

The hint of emotion disappeared as swiftly as it had appeared, replaced by something hard and unsettling. Not the affable, immature playboy, but the man who had brought Cabrera Shipping back from the brink of ruin. An intelligent, driven man who, she was finding out the hard way, went after what he wanted.

What did it say about her, that instead of being angry or afraid, a thrill shot through her veins at the sight of that strength?

"You agreed to spend time with me, Calandra. To get to know me better. A three-hour train ride by yourself is not the way to accomplish that."

"You canceled my ticket," she repeated.

"Of course. How rude of me. Next time I'll just let you pay for a ticket you're not going to use."

She didn't know which was worse—that he had interfered in her travel plans and was showing absolutely no remorse, or that he was at least partially right. When he'd brought up traveling to Marseille as he escorted her back to her bed-and-breakfast after their trip to the Eiffel Tower, she'd interrupted him with a plea of a headache and rushed inside, away from what she'd known would be his suggestion that they travel together.

Before she stuck her foot in her mouth or, worse, apologized, she started to climb the stairs into the plane. A hand settled on her waist, and she bit back a gasp as electricity skipped across her skin and sent frissons of crackling warmth straight to her thighs. She turned and nearly came nose to nose with Alejandro. He stood on the step behind her, but with his impressive height, they were face-to-face. He kept his hand at her waist, his touch burning through the thin cloth of her dress.

Could he hear her heartbeat as it galloped through her chest? Did he see the rise and fall of her breasts as she tried to keep her breathing steady?

Slowly, ever so slowly, his fingers trailed from her hip, delicious, traitorous shivers radiating from his fingertips throughout her body.

And then he laid his hand flat across her belly. Possession tightened his face as his lips parted and his eyes grew dark. She was caught in a whirlwind of conflicting desires—the need to run away, far away, and the desire to lean in, to let go of her control and let him in.

"This child is ours, Calandra." He leaned in, and for one brief, horrific, glorious moment, she thought he was going to kiss her. "Ours."

Before she could gather her wildly spinning thoughts and utter a retort, a voice called out from behind her.

"Ready to leave in five, Monsieur Cabrera."

She turned away and walked up the stairs with measured steps. She wasn't going to give him the satisfaction of letting him see how much his touch, his words, had unsettled her.

She entered the plane, trying to ignore the mahogany wood floors, beige leather seats and computer screens installed in the back of each chair. A dim memory of flying in a similar plane when she was eight surfaced, her mother sitting limply toward the front and her father in back behind a curtain. When she'd sneaked out of her seat and peeked behind the curtain, it had been to see her father with his hands buried in the gold curls of the flight attendant as he'd kissed her.

Nausea rolled in her stomach. She quickened her pace, determined to get to her seat before she made a fool of herself.

And then stopped at the sight of the robin's egg–blue package tied up with silver string sitting in one of the seats.

She glanced over her shoulder. "For me?"

Alejandro dropped into a chair and propped his feet up on the seat of another across the aisle. A casual move, but one that made her feel trapped. No last mad dash to the exit before they closed the doors.

"Perhaps."

She rolled her eyes and leaned down to read the gift tag attached to the outrageous bow.

A mi bebe.

Her throat tightened. Her heart followed suit. *For my baby.* The passion Alejandro had displayed yesterday, his desire to be involved in their child's life, this… He'd shown more interest in the little one growing inside her in the last twenty-four hours than her father ever had in his own children.

Swallowing her emotions, she picked up the box and turned. "Should I save it for the baby to open?"

Alejandro grinned. "I dare you to wait that long."

With a shake of her head, she undid the bow and

lifted the lid. Nestled inside among white and blue wrapping paper lay a chestnut-colored teddy bear with blue paws that matched the gift box and a silver heart around its neck.

The simple gift touched her. She hadn't bought the baby any toys. Her fingers glided over the soft fur as she lifted it out of the box, then rested on the silver script on one of the bear's feet.

Recognizing the luxury brand, she looked back at Alejandro. "These cost almost a thousand dollars."

He shrugged. "I'm rich. I want our child to have the best."

Her heart sank. He wasn't her father, no. But he still rated things by how much they cost, placed value on the price tag instead of the intrinsic value. If her child were anything like Johanna, the teddy bear would be covered in sand and dampened by the ocean air in no time. The baby wouldn't care if the teddy bear had cost five dollars or five thousand.

"What's wrong?" Alejandro asked as she sat.

"Nothing."

She didn't like that he could read her so easily. Sometimes Aunt Norine and even Johanna had trouble discerning her moods. She'd liked it that way. Smooth, unreadable, unflappable. Less room for mistakes, for heartache, when you kept yourself locked up so tight no one could penetrate.

"Something's stirring behind those daggers in your eyes." He nodded at the bear. "Not expensive enough?"

She sat, the bear cradled carefully on her lap, as another possibility crept in, ugly and insidious. The limo, the fancy jet, the expensive gift…he'd said he wasn't going to buy access to their child. But his actions said otherwise.

A flight attendant came by and set a drink on her table, green and frothy with a sprig of mint perched across the rim of the glass.

"Oh, I can't—"

"It's a virgin mojito, Mademoiselle Smythe," she said with a smile. "Monsieur Cabrera provided us with your dietary restrictions and preferences this morning. But please let us know if there's anything else you require."

Calandra glanced at her watch as the flight attendant waltzed down the length of the plane, keeping her gaze on Alejandro out of the corner of her eye. To his credit, he didn't even glance at the woman's hips swaying beneath her tight skirt.

"Cocktails before noon?" she asked as the flight attendant returned and set before him a highball glass with thin ribbon of amber liquid at the bottom.

"Ten thirty here is three thirty in the morning in New York." He shot her a heated smile. "I recall both of us having a refreshing beverage around that time."

Oh, yes. He'd ordered champagne after their first bout of lovemaking. They'd sipped it in bed as he demanded she share something she'd never told anyone else. Her quip that she'd already given him her virginity had made him smile, but he hadn't relented, pressing until she'd revealed her early-morning walks on the beach and the collection of shells beneath her bed. Silly, but a ritual she'd developed her first summer living with Aunt Norine.

She should have known then, the way he hadn't let her pull away, that he was so much *more*. But she'd been in a first-time-sex-induced haze of euphoria, not paying attention to the warning signs like the tug on her heart.

Shrugging off the memories, she grabbed her mojito glass, took a sip and moaned. Her eyes drifted shut as the tart taste of lime mingled with the soothing scent of mint. She'd never thought to make herself virgin cocktails, but she'd have to make this a part of her evening routine. Utterly relaxing.

Her eyes opened, and she nearly choked. Alejandro's eyes were fixed on her, blazing with intense desire.

And then it was gone, so quick she wondered if her own traitorous body had conjured up the image.

Apparently, pregnancy did not inhibit her libido.

"Tasty?"

"Yes, thank you." She'd had her one night with Alejandro, just like dozens of women before her. If she ever entertained the possibility of succumbing to temptation again, all she had to do was conjure up the paparazzi photos of Alejandro getting out of a limo with that slim, dark-haired actress in a clingy red dress in the same week she'd found out she was pregnant.

The reminder dashed a much-needed splash of cold water on her passion.

"Tell me more about this project." Business was a safe topic. "I understand wanting *La Reina* to be a success, but you mentioned something else."

"Ah, yes." Alejandro laughed, the sound unexpectedly harsh. "If the board doesn't accept my proposal, I will be replaced as head of Cabrera Shipping."

"What? By whom?"

Alejandro's smile was so sharp it could have cut glass.

"My father."

CHAPTER NINE

CALANDRA'S EYES WIDENED, just a fraction, but enough to show her surprise.

God, he'd missed this. Four months of no witty banter, no gray eyes snapping at him, no cool retorts that heated his blood. Compared to the uncertainty regarding Cabrera Shipping's future and his father's threats, Calandra's familiar presence, not to mention her incredible revelation, were rays of light warming him during one of the most challenging times of his life.

His eyes drifted down once more to her stomach. In five months, he would meet his child.

His child. He hadn't really contemplated having children before. His casual romances and liaisons had excluded that type of commitment, one even more binding than a marriage license. Most probably assumed his first thought would have been horror.

Surprisingly, the more he'd thought about it after their conversation yesterday, reflected on Calandra's dream of taking their child to the top of the Eiffel Tower, the chief emotion had been wonder. Wonder and excitement.

However, he reminded himself, only if the woman across from him would let him be a part of their child's life. Yes, he could absolutely throw his weight around, hire lawyers and drag her to court. And if he had to, he would.

But that was something his father would do. Wowing, charming or even seducing what he wanted from Calandra was preferable to following in his father's footsteps in any fashion.

The thought of Javier taking away the one thing he'd dedicated himself to, the company he'd literally poured blood and sweat into, made his chest burn with the same fury he'd felt the day he'd discovered Javier in the library with his cheating bitch.

Now, though, it wasn't Javier's threats and attempts to control his life that pushed him. The determination to be the father Javier never had been added a light to the darkness. Even if Cabrera Shipping fell apart, he'd have a son or daughter. He'd fought for Cabrera Shipping, poured his soul into something for the first time in years. But it was something that had been gifted to him, a scrap thrown to the mongrel of the family. *La Reina* was the first thing in his life that would be his. Yet Javier had even managed to taint that with his interference.

The baby was the first thing he'd cared about that his father couldn't take away from him. And he'd be damned if he was going to let Calandra keep him from his child.

Alejandro grinned at Calandra, his casual smile hiding his turmoil. By the end of this week, she'd agree to his terms.

"Your father wants to head Cabrera Shipping?"

Her cold question snapped him out of his erotic musings. Anyone would have thought her completely in control, ivory skin so smooth and pale she could have been carved from marble.

Only he saw the drum of her fingers on her thigh, the pulse beating just below the elegant curve of her jaw.

"Yes."

A tiny V appeared between her brows. "Why? Doesn't he already oversee multiple other businesses?"

He glanced down at his drink, his muscles tightening as the memory of that phone call echoed in his head.

"Cabrera Shipping is losing money, Alejandro. Fix it." A heavy sigh. *"Or I'll have to fix it for you."*

"I mentioned we're behind on construction, yes?"

"Yes. Two ships?"

"Yes. By about a month on one and three on another. It may not seem like much, but four weeks behind means two to three trips down the drain. Millions upon millions of dollars in cargo going to other shippers."

"I'm sorry."

"Thank you. Unfortunate," he added with a flippancy he didn't feel. "But the loss has, understandably, made stakeholders and the board nervous. Convincing them to spend more money on renovating an aging ship when we just lost so much and saw clients move, at least temporarily, to other companies is not an easy feat." He leaned into the plush cushions of his seat and closed his eyes as the enormity of the task before him weighed on his shoulders. "My father, the majority stakeholder, does not support the alternative use of *La Reina*. He holds considerable influence over the board. If they vote no on this proposal, Cabrera Shipping will no longer be mine."

"That seems harsh."

He shrugged, the casual gesture masking decades of pain. "He's not a kind man. I see the loss in revenue as a temporary setback. He sees it as a catastrophic blow to our bottom line. Not that he was a fan of my idea about *La Reina* to begin with. In his mind it's further evidence that I have no head for business. I'm squandering company finances to create a playground for the rich."

Sentiments his father had expressed multiple times over the last few weeks. Thankfully, the comments had been delivered over the phone so Javier couldn't see the effect his lack of faith had on his middle son.

Ridiculous, really. Alejandro loathed his father. Had for over twenty years now. His opinion shouldn't matter.

Silence. At last, he opened his eyes. Calandra stared out the window at the ground passing by, one hand resting lightly on her belly.

Despite the warmth of the afternoon, she wore her customary black. Slashes of black eyeliner reminded him of war paint instead of makeup.

Still, she'd softened since he'd last seen her. He'd first glimpsed it on the Eiffel Tower yesterday, but now he saw it in more vivid detail. Perhaps it was the gentle curve of her lips as her fingers traced back and forth over her stomach. Or maybe it was the occasional flashes of emotion he caught on her face, glimpses into the woman who'd seduced him with her intelligence and no-nonsense attitude.

"Why do you want to repurpose *La Reina*?"

An innocent question he wanted to answer glibly.

But she sounded like she truly wanted to know, a notion that made his chest swell with pride.

"*La Reina* was the first ship I sailed on when I took over." He could still taste the salt of the sea the first time the bow had carved through the waves of the Atlantic. His first bit of freedom from the confines of the persona he'd trapped himself in. "Helped out on the crew to understand how everything worked. She's thirty years old, which is ancient in cargo ship years. But it's hard to picture the old girl being sailed off to a graveyard and stripped down to nothing."

"That's an expensive endeavor for the sake of nostalgia."

"Nostalgia's part of it," he conceded. "But I want Cabrera Shipping to go in a new direction. Our latest ships are being constructed to meet new environmental standards. I want *La Reina* to be a part of that trend, not contributing to waste but being reused."

An unexpected wistfulness crossed Calandra's face. "I wasn't expecting that sort of viewpoint from someone so…"

"So what?"

Naked pain flashed in her eyes before she shut down, misty silver shifting to steel gray in a heartbeat. Her fingers clenched around the armrest for the briefest of moments before he saw her intentionally relax her body and recline back.

"Someone who views people as inconsequential, playthings to be discarded when they cease being interesting."

The harsh remark hit him hard. He started to retort, to snap out a comment that both covered his pain and delivered a blow of his own, but stopped. Unlike his father, her words weren't designed to hurt. They were coming from a different place, something rooted in Calandra's past.

"Do you truly think that of me?"

She continued to stare, so intensely that he had to stop himself from shifting in his seat beneath her perusal.

"I don't know what to think," she finally said. The coldness slipped, and he got a glimpse of vulnerability in the crinkling of her eyes, the little V between her brows. "One minute I think I have you figured out and the next…"

She blinked and the vulnerability disappeared. "Tell me more about the event. What you want to accomplish, what you envision, what still needs to be done."

So, he did. He talked for what felt like forever, though a glance at his watch revealed it had only been thirty minutes or so. No one, not even the board members who supported *La Reina*, had shown as much interest as Calandra did.

It was unsettling, the way she watched him so attentively. Like she could see everything about him. The women he'd dated the past year had been the exact opposite. They'd never looked past his money, the fancy cars or the glamorous vacations he whisked them off to on his private jet.

However, no matter how much he was embracing this new phase of life, he had no desire to invite a woman into it permanently. As far as the world knew, he was having too much too fun to settle down.

Let them think whatever they like.

Being a father to their child would enable him to step up and be a parent the way Javier had never been.

But marriage…no one, not even his parents, had managed to maintain a true and loving relationship. His mother didn't know it, but she was married to a lie.

He didn't want to even tempt that kind of fate. Nor, that nasty little voice in his head whispered, did he want to risk the other possibility.

That he was more like his father than he wanted to admit. That one woman would never be enough.

"Before you dive in, you need to see the ship." He glanced out the window and spied the deep blue waters of the Mediterranean on the horizon. "We're close. Once we land, I've arranged for you to tour *La Reina*."

"Good idea. Who's giving me the tour?" she asked.

He grinned. "Me."

An hour later, he watched Calandra as she circled around the ballroom for what had to be the ninth time. Eyes flickering over every last detail, her face revealing nothing.

He glanced over the ballroom. Most of the floor had been done in white marble flecked with gray, with a light gray wood for the dance floor in the middle. White columns soared up to the ceiling. A custom, hand-blown glass chandelier dominated the room, casting a warm glow over the tables below.

The all white had not been his first choice. Adrian's dining room in Paris was all white. Boring. Flat. Interesting to see how long that color scheme lasted once his and Everleigh's child started running around.

But here…here it screamed elegance. Wealth. Power.

Even if the board voted against this endeavor and Javier yanked Cabrera Shipping away from him, he would make *La Reina* a success. Everyone, including his father, thought he squandered his money. Few knew that ever since he'd taken over a year after college, he'd stashed away most of his profits in a Swiss bank account. He'd spend every last dime he had until the very end if he had to.

Well, almost every last dime, he amended as he glanced again at Calandra. Hiring her had solved two problems—knowing his event was in good hands and finding a way to get her to accept money. He'd had a private investigator look into her circumstances. He knew she and her sister were living in a tiny house in a little town on the coast. He knew the exact amount of her bank account. Her savings, while admirable, would barely cover her medical bills and living expenses through the end of the year.

Stubborn woman.

"It's beautiful," she said as she joined him.

Having her approval shouldn't affect him. But it did. *"Gracias."*

"I have an appointment tomorrow with the caterer to confirm details. Then Thursday for final planning and evaluation—"

"And hopefully some time in there for us to spend together."

Her brows drew together. "What?"

"We're supposed to be getting to know each other. Not in the biblical sense, of course, since we already checked that box."

"Twice," she replied dryly with that so-sexy arched brow. But sadly, the flirtatious glint disappeared as quickly as it had unexpectedly appeared. "I have a lot of work to do, Alejandro."

"I'll accompany you."

She held up a hand. "No. I work best alone."

He frowned. Being told no was not something he was used to. Nor, he acknowledged as his jaw tightened, did he like it.

"Dinner, then. This week."

The narrowing of her eyes indicated a protest was incoming.

"I insist."

She chewed on her lower lip, a gesture of consternation but one that nonetheless conjured images of her naked, stretched across his bed and watching him not with an icy gaze but a hot stare that demanded he come over, strip off his clothes and join her.

It had been way too long since he'd had sex.

"Fine."

She turned and started toward the exit. For some reason, the sight of her walking away nicked his pride. He caught up to her in several swift strides.

"Where are you going?"

"Into Marseille. I have a lot of work to do."

"You do know most of the vendors have phone numbers. There's no need to traipse around and tire yourself. I can take you back, or," he added testily, "if you've tired of my company, I can send for the limo."

She stopped so quickly and turned around that he nearly careened into her.

And then they were close. Too close.

"I don't need your limo." Her voice was eerily calm, devoid of emotion, as was the rest of her countenance.

Save her eyes. Those glittered with some emotion he couldn't discern. Normally he could read women with astonishing accuracy. It's why they enjoyed him so much. He knew, and gave, exactly what they wanted.

What did Calandra Smythe want?

He watched her for a moment, eyes sliding down the curve of her neck, the slenderness of her waist, although now as he looked closer he saw the tiniest swell beneath her black dress.

That's my child.

The thought simultaneously thrilled and terrified him. He wanted to be a part of that child's life more than anything. But could he do it? Could he be a better father than his own?

"I was very successful when I worked for Cabrera Wines," Calandra replied testily. "That is why you hired me, right?"

"Of course."

"Not because you're trying to pad my bank account?"

"I would never be so underhanded."

She stared at him for a long, long moment. Then leaned in closer.

He went hard. Almost instantly. His eyes caressed her smooth, pale face, the column of her neck, the enticing place where her pulse pounded at the base of her throat…

His gaze snapped up. Calandra Smythe was just as affected as he was. Her pupils dilated as a slow smile curved across his face. Her lips parted. Her quick intake of breath sent heat careening through his veins.

"Let me do my job, Alejandro." Her words came out breathy this time, all sense of calm laid waste by the attraction crackling between them. "And for the rest of the day, please leave me alone."

She turned away again and started for the door. This time, he didn't pursue. The uncharted territories of parenthood and interest in a woman beyond her body were unfamiliar and uncomfortable.

But the game of seduction was one he knew very well.

He had one week. One week to impress, to woo, to get her to agree not only to let him be involved in their child's life, but to perhaps have her in his bed once more. The thought of feeling her body beneath him, of the novelty of making love to the woman who carried his child within her, made him positively giddy.

"Your wish is my command."

She didn't respond, didn't even acknowledge she'd heard him, as she disappeared into the main corridor.

Unexpected parenthood. His company on the brink of being torn from his grasp. His arrogant bastard of a father still interfering in his life. With all the uncertainty, and all the things that could possibly go wrong, he should have felt concerned, on edge, nervous.

All that paled in comparison to the memory of that sharp intake of breath.

His smile grew wider still. In one week, he would achieve his desires. Cabrera Shipping. *La Reina*. His child.

And Calandra Smythe in his bed.

CHAPTER TEN

CALANDRA WATCHED THE boats drifting across the waters of the Vieux-Port de Marseille from her spot at a little café with red-and-white-striped umbrellas. The scent of fresh-baked bread had guided her feet to this little haven as she killed time before her appointment.

The city was a welcome distraction from the luxury of Alejandro's seaside villa. The teal-blue furniture, floor-to-ceiling windows and her own private guest quarters at the end of a long hallway had screamed wealth. Only one thing had stood out as truly Alejandro among the carefully chosen name-brand items—artsy photographs of ships, from the historic floating palaces of the early twentieth century to romantic sailboats, tucked here and there among more recognizable pieces.

A far cry from the tiny house Aunt Norine had raised her and Johanna in. A reminder of everything Alejandro was, no matter how charming or seductive he could be.

Pride had made her take a cab to the villa yesterday afternoon once she realized that there really wasn't a lot to be done in town. She'd managed to work successfully at a table on the patio, surrounded by lush blooms and the greenest grass she'd ever seen as she confirmed vendors and created schedules.

It had been heaven working again. Feeling useful. And this morning, when her first emergency had arisen, she'd thrilled at making last-minute arrangements to put out what had the potential to be a very large fire.

One more step, two more steps at most, and *La Reina*'s party would be back on track.

Would Alejandro be proud of her quick response and her unique solution?

She shoved away the unwelcome thought. She didn't need his approval. She had done her job just fine without begging for compliments and praise before. No need to start now.

The *garçon* came out and set a plate with a fluffy croissant, wild berry jam and a tiny bowl of fruit on the table with a flourish.

"Pour vous, mademoiselle."

"Merci."

She reached for the knife when nausea hit so hard she could barely move.

"Oh, baby, what are you doing to me?" she whispered. Already she loved the little one growing inside her so much. But moments like these, she could do without.

The nausea slowly subsided, and she sat back in her chair, her breathing heavy, her forehead damp. A long drink of water further settled her stomach.

Maybe a combination of pregnancy and concern. Concern that she was headed down the same path as Mother. She'd tossed and turned a good portion of the night as she replayed the scene on *La Reina* over and over again, trying to figure out how she'd let go of her control and let him see that he still affected her.

The exhaustion that invaded her bones could be chalked up to the energy her body required to grow her child. But there was no excuse for the fragility she'd developed. Her child needed her to be the strong woman she'd been for the last seventeen years.

She grabbed the knife once more and slathered jam on the croissant. She bit into it, savoring the sweet burst of berries on her tongue, and sighed. At least one thing had gone right today. Nothing beat the simple pleasures of eating a freshly baked French croissant.

"Does the baby have a sweet tooth?"

She choked on the croissant and coughed. Someone pressed a glass of water into her hand. She brought it to her lips and gulped it down.

Alejandro dropped into the chair across from her. A frown marred his handsome features. The sleeves of his brick-red polo shirt clung to his biceps, the blue jeans conforming to his thighs. Irritation buzzed inside her head. Did the man always have to look so put together?

"Are you all right?"

Gulls cawed overhead. Languages from around the world flowing around them in a bewitching hymn of sounds and accents as shoppers and tourists bustled by. A breeze blew in from the harbor, light and cool to combat the growing heat of the morning. Details Calandra would have soaked up in her new quest to enjoy life a little more had her mutinous body not gone rigid the instant it registered Alejandro's presence.

"Are you having me followed?" she replied. She kept her voice neutral, even though his banal question put her guard up. A normal person might think his interest sweet. But to her, it was the top of a very slippery slope. One where she let herself be lured in by his supposed kindness, gifts and, damn it, desire, only to have the rug yanked out from under her when he got bored.

It's what men like him did.

A light breeze stirred his hair. The knot in her chest twisted painfully. Was this what it was like for her mother? Fingers aching to touch the man who stirred such powerful emotions in her? Knowing all along that the more she gave him, the harder she'd fall when he left?

Because men like her father—like Alejandro—didn't stay. They never stayed.

Alejandro pointed toward the bay, where a yacht gently bobbed next to one of the docks. Even from this distance, she could see the name painted in bright red letters.

"La Pimpinela Escarlata?"

"Your Spanish is very good."

"Not good enough. *Escarlata* is 'scarlet,' but *pimpinela*?"

"The scarlet pimpernel. A plant with scarlet flowers." His lips quirked up at the corners. "Also the name of a movie I watched with Madre as a child."

The name teased her memory. "Isn't it a book, too?"

"One of the few times I have enjoyed the movie more than the book. Featuring a devastatingly handsome hero with a flair for fashion and seduction."

"I didn't know you liked to read."

"There are a lot of things you don't know about me." He tapped his hand on the table. "Which is why, when my yacht docked and I spied a woman in black seated at a bayside café, I decided to take advantage so we could spend a little time together."

An emphatic *No!* sounded from her more rational mind. Her heart, that useless muscle that had gone from iron-clad and frosty to weak and feeling, disagreed.

"Alejandro—"

"Calandra," he broke in, "you set the terms of this arrangement." He leaned across the table and, before she could stop him, grabbed her hand in his. "And you're avoiding me." His finger traced a circle on the back of her hand, his delicate touch as light as butterfly wings, yet no less potent than the sensual attack he'd unleashed on her body four months ago. "I just want to get to know you better."

The pattern he'd traced on her skin burned as if he'd etched it into her. She snapped her gaze off his hand and refocused on her half-eaten croissant.

"Which leaves me with only one course of action. To show the mother of my child that I'm not the evil man she thinks I am."

She sighed. "You're not evil. I never accused you of that."

He glanced toward the bay, his hand staying on top of hers as if he was afraid she might flee.

Which she had. Multiple times. But in this moment, running was the furthest thing from her mind. What was first and forefront was the hint of discomfort she'd heard in his voice.

"I don't think you're evil," she repeated. She tugged her hand out, but before he could move settled her fingers on top of his. Warmth blossomed in her fingertips as she registered the slight dusting of black hair on the back of his hand, the heat of his skin, the erotic contrast of dark tan skin beneath her own pale white.

"Then why?"

When he turned to look at her, there was no arousal in his eyes. No artifice, no seduction. Just a simple question and, if she looked a little deeper, pain lurking in those dark blue depths.

She had no desire to air her family's deepest secrets. But the longer she looked at Alejandro, *really* looked at him, the guiltier she felt. Yes, he was a playboy. Unlike her father, however, she'd never seen evidence of him being cruel, of using money to try and slap a Band-Aid over a heart he'd crushed to smithereens with his selfishness.

"My father...he liked to have fun. Too much fun." Her mind raced as she tried to condense years of pain, rage and loss into as few words as possible. "His actions, especially his infidelity, hurt my mother. To the point that she became very depressed and eventually passed away."

A simplified and very watered-down version of the truth. But it was the best she could manage for now.

"I'm sorry."

She swallowed hard and nodded. "Thank you." She sat back, pulling her hand away. The moment of reassurance had been nice, but the longer she allowed it, the more likely she was to share more. Sharing led to vulnerability. Vulnerability led to feelings. In her experience, feelings led to heartbreaking situations like a young girl being forced to grow up into a mother and caregiver before her tenth birthday.

Or two daughters watching their mother's coffin

being lowered into the ground, one still just a child, the other forced into adulthood far too fast.

But, she reminded herself as she put the brakes on her maudlin reminiscing, the genuine empathy in Alejandro's eyes let her know she'd done the right thing. If he was truly interested in being a father to their child, he deserved to know why she was struggling so hard with letting him be a part of her life.

Johanna would be proud, she thought wryly. Her sister was always encouraging her to open up and share her feelings more.

"I better understand your reticence to let me into our child's life." He leaned back in his chair. "One thing I'd like to reassure you on, Calandra. I won't be parading women in and out of their life. I want him, or her, to have some stability."

She swallowed the insult that rose in her throat, harsh words powered by bias and an unwelcome bit of jealousy.

"Thank you."

"What can I do to make you feel more comfortable with the idea of me being involved?"

A small smile tugged at her lips. "Just you asking makes me feel a little better. My father didn't have an interest in my mother's opinion."

"Your opinion matters a great deal, Calandra."

There was magic in those words. Powerful, seductive magic coupled with a devastatingly handsome man who wanted to be a father to her child.

"Then we'll find opportunities to get to know each other better over the next few days." She nodded toward the myriad of streets and shops that lay just beyond the port's edge. "I have a one o'clock with a prospective caterer."

Alejandro frowned. "I already had a caterer lined up."

"A caterer whose owner was tossed in jail last night for driving drunk and is now facing a PR nightmare." She set enough euros on the table to cover her bill and stood. "You're welcome to walk with me if you'd like."

Five minutes later, they strolled down one of the many charming alleys Marseille had to offer. A casual walk with at least three feet of distance between them. It didn't stop every nerve ending in her body from sizzling.

"Who do you have in mind to replace my caterer?" Alejandro asked.

She started to respond, excitement humming at the prospect of finding the perfect vendor who fit seamlessly into the plan.

Until a flash of sunshine caught her eye.

She couldn't help it; her head jerked around. There in the window of a small boutique was the most exquisite gown she'd ever seen. Buttery yellow and sleeveless, with a sweetheart bodice that followed the curves of the mannequin like a lover's hand, layer upon layer of gauzy skirt that fell to the floor...

A dream. A dress that would make any girl feel like a princess.

She looked away. Not her. She'd never been a princess. Efficient, professional, all work and no play. That was Calandra Smythe.

"Calandra?"

She blinked and looked away, continuing forward.

"Sorry. For the catering…"

Her voice trailed off as Alejandro's hand settled on her shoulder.

"What?"

His eyes searched, probed, delving so deep she barely resisted squirming under the intensity of his gaze.

"What?"

"The dress."

"It's just a dress."

"It may be just a dress, but you do have a special event coming up. Something other than black, perhaps."

"Black is a versatile color."

His eyes narrowed thoughtfully. "You know, I don't think I've ever seen you in anything other than black. Well," he added, his voice lowering and making her stomach flip-flop, "once."

She refused to blush. "I like black."

"Yes, but why?"

She barely resisted squirming under his scrutiny. No one had ever asked why before. Everyone else had just labeled her as falling into the goth phase or joked that she must attend a lot of funerals. One young man she'd rejected in college had said she dressed in the same color as her soul. Dramatic and petulant, but the comment still crept under her skin. Johanna and Aunt Norine were the only ones who knew that to her black meant armor. Strength. Security. It had since the day of Mother's funeral, when she'd walked into her father's study in her black mourning dress and wielded power over him for the first time in her life.

"I just do."

"You hide so much of yourself."

With a deep breath, she turned and met his gaze head-on. "Spoken like someone who also hides behind a mask."

He jerked back. Surprise flashed in his eyes. Then it disappeared as he gave her one of those insincere smiles.

"Touché. So are you going to try it on?"

"It's not me."

Pride, and a little bit of shame, refused to let her admit that she wanted to try on the dress very badly.

Her phone beeped. She glanced down and sucked in a relieved breath. "Five minutes until my appointment."

She took off down the boulevard, her pace quick, not giving him enough time to reply. He caught up to her, his long legs eating up the distance she'd put between them. They walked in uneasy silence, passing more shops and cafés, until a violet-colored sign with white lettering caught her eye. She slowed her pace.

"Here we are."

He glanced up at the sign and frowned.

"Le Giordano École Culinaire. A culinary school? I thought you were going to meet with a caterer."

She held up her phone. "I am. Suzanne Giordano's culinary school offers catering."

His frown deepened. "Maybe I didn't make my wishes clear. This event has to impress some of the richest men in the world to not only continue to invest in *La Reina*, but let me keep Cabrera Shipping. Burned bread and attempts at an appetizer some kid saw online won't cut it."

Her heart thumped hard again, but this time in anger.

"Spoken like a spoiled billionaire."

He leaned in, eyes narrowing, that dangerous intensity she'd glimpsed back in Paris on full display.

"You don't know a thing about me."

"Judging by your elitist comment, I know all I need to know," she snapped back. "Your brother trusted me implicitly, and every event I executed for Cabrera Wines was a success. You said you trusted me. Clearly you don't."

"I don't trust a bunch of aspiring chefs who might give my guests food poisoning."

She punched in a website on her phone and held the screen up to his face. "Suzie Giordano has trained multiple two- and three-star Michelin chefs. She's won awards all around the world. The chef who cooked your fancy meal in London a few months ago is a graduate of her school."

His handsome features hardened until it looked like his face had been chiseled out of granite.

"London?" Silky menace laced the word. "How did you know about London?"

"Don't flatter yourself." She swallowed her bitterness. "I didn't stalk you. I didn't have to. There were photos everywhere." Somehow, she managed to keep her voice from cracking underneath the weight of her pain. Which was worse? The sharp sting of remembering how quickly her one and only lover had replaced her? Or the icy fingers of memory clutching her heart and squeezing as the echoes of her mother's sobs at discovering yet another mistress played over and over in her head?

"London wasn't what you think."

"Of course it wasn't." She waved a hand. "But it's

not important anyway. What is important is that you're questioning my ability to do a job you hired me for."

He blew out a breath and ran a frustrated hand through his curls. "Calandra, this is not—"

"Perhaps," she interrupted, "if you don't trust me, I should go home."

Nothing. Absolute silence as he stared at her, eyes blank, face smooth, without the slightest hint of expression.

Like looking in a mirror.

Was this what people saw when they talked to her? The thought made her sick to her stomach. It would have been better to see something, anything.

Anything but complete and utter disinterest. Because this was what she feared seeing. A month, six months, a year. Whenever the allure of this novelty wore off, this would be the look she'd see.

Although perhaps it was better to see it now. Remind herself that he might be able to shove his way into their child's life legally. But that didn't mean she had to let him into hers. And she would move heaven and earth to keep her son or daughter from having to see that same look on his face, from ever falling into the trap their grandmother had of wondering if they just weren't enough.

She turned and continued down the road. She didn't look back. If he didn't trust her, better to cut the cord now before she got any deeper.

CHAPTER ELEVEN

CALANDRA CUPPED HER hands around her mug of tea as she watched the waves crash along the beach. The rising sun warmed her skin as she relaxed at what she'd come to think of as her table on the patio. Sea salt danced on the air. The perfect setting for rest and relaxation.

Or it would have been if her damn heart would stop kicking into overdrive every time she thought she heard someone approach. Even though her time at the culinary school had served as a welcome distraction, Alejandro had been ever-present in her mind, intruding and refusing to let her eject him from her thoughts. Already she'd made a mistake; she'd lowered her defenses at the harbor, on their walk. She'd taken the olive branch he'd offered too easily. Had it been his simple, sweet plea that he wanted to get to know her better? Or the feeling of his hand rubbing circles on the back of her hand and stirring memories of that same hand closing over her breast with a possessive heat?

Whatever it was, she'd caved. Not five minutes later, he'd shown that he didn't trust her, that money was more important than anything else and, worst of all, that once something or someone challenged him, he shut them out.

She'd entertained the idea of calling his bluff and booking a flight back to North Carolina. But she'd be running away, tail between her legs, and merely putting off a battle that would turn into a full-scale legal war.

So she'd forced herself to carry on yesterday. She'd spent nearly three hours at the school, a three-story building with creamy blue walls covered with photos of beaming graduates and colorful culinary concoctions. Her mood had been significantly bolstered, partially because of the delectable food and partially because of the energetic company of Suzie Giordano, a short woman with a long silver braid draped over one shoulder and a booming voice. The crinkles etched into her skin that told a story of years of smiling and laughter had reminded Calandra of Aunt Norine. She'd relaxed almost instantly and even smiled back.

Suzie had given her a tour of the school, weaving in and out of the classes in session, providing tips to eager students and the occasional joke in rapid-fire French. By the time she'd sat Calandra down at a small table on the balcony on the third floor, she was almost certain that she'd found the right place. One bite of canapés Lorenzo had settled it, savoring the taste of the crispy parmesan cheese and hearty crabmeat.

Part of what had made her so successful as an event planner, especially in New York, had been her ability to identify talent and solidify new relationships. She had known as soon as she'd seen the arrangement at a floral show that the girl who'd dropped out of college would be the next sought-after florist. She'd locked in an exclusive deal with a string quartet made up of a schoolteacher, a retired army colonel and twins who ran a bookstore in SoHo.

Most would have laughed at the notion that Calandra Smythe, the ice queen herself, was capable of building relationships. When it came to the billionaires and lofty business professionals she'd worked with, that was absolutely true.

But when it came to the people those billionaires and professionals looked down on, she thrived. Her blunt words, her loyalty to those who showed up and did their job, had made her successful.

Calandra glanced up. Nine o'clock in the morning as the sun climbed higher into the Mediterranean sky. In Kitty Hawk the moon would still be up, turning the surface of the ocean into an ethereal silver that lit up her attic bedroom.

Ever since finding out about the baby, she'd looked at Aunt Norine's house with new eyes. While it had been a refuge after her mother's funeral, she'd resisted calling it "home." Now, thousands of miles away, she longed for the creaky porch and the worn but stark white lace curtains that hung in the windows.

Lace curtains that, despite their overly bleached, frayed appearance, reminded her of the gauzy curtains hanging in the suite in New York, filtering the streetlights and casting shifting shadows over Alejandro's incredible body as they'd made love.

Another memory blazed forth before she could stop it. The night of the party in New York, when four members of the cleaning crew had failed to show, she'd kicked off her heels, grabbed a trash bag and started cleaning up. It had been just after midnight, she'd been exhausted and had wanted nothing more than to crawl in bed.

She'd turned after clearing one of the tables and nearly run into Alejandro, sleeves of his dress shirt rolled up, tie undone and hanging around his neck.

"What can I do?"

Those four words had rocked the foundation of who she thought him to be. He stayed for two hours, helping her pack away centerpieces, toss tablecloths into laundry baskets and, just as they'd been about to call it a night, had taken the mop he'd been wielding and performed a tango across the ballroom floor.

She'd laughed. He'd grinned, not a playboy's smirk but a friendly, heart-melting smile that had heated her blood. They'd gotten into the elevator. Who moved first, she'd never know. They'd crashed into each other, drawn in by the power of a desire they'd been suppressing for years that had suddenly burst free and claimed them in one soul-altering kiss.

The man he'd been that night was the man her heart remembered. The man she could accept, even embrace, as the father of her child.

Although the more he talked about *La Reina*, the more he revealed of himself, the more she remembered their interactions over the years, how she'd started to become aware when he walked into a room or even looked forward to the conversations they'd have.

Was the man she'd started to see real? Or an illusion?

Doesn't matter. He doesn't trust you, her brain reminded her with cruel honesty.

Adrian had trusted her. Yes, he'd required evidence, plans, documentation. When she'd suggested an ap-

petizer for the last release party that included BBQ
sauce, she'd had to show him sales of the condiment
in the United States and the recipe she'd obtained from
a famous chef.

But he'd trusted her. Alejandro, on the other hand,
only cared about impressing his board.

For one brief moment, when he'd tried to persuade
her to try on the dress, she thought he'd seen something most people missed. That she had dreams, hopes,
desires, beyond her career. That she exuded coldness
because, ever since her mother's passing, she'd had to,
to stay sane, to stay strong for Johanna.

Stupid. If she just clung to the memories of him
with his parade of women, the overly cheery insults
he'd lobbed at her over the years, she could keep him
at arm's length.

"How was the food?" His husky voice interrupted
her thoughts. Her heart jumped, but her hands stayed
steady on her tea mug. She could do this.

"Delicious," she replied. "Too bad you missed it."

He circled the table and walked into her line of sight.

She'd only ever thought of food as delicious before.
But the sight of Alejandro clad only in navy swim
shorts that clung to his perfectly muscled backside had
her rethinking the term.

Sun gleamed off his tan skin. Her eyes ran over his
chest, the dark hair that trailed down his stomach and
disappeared into the waistband of his trunks. Despite
the dark-colored fabric, the bulge between his thighs
wasn't hard to miss.

Her head snapped up in time to see his satisfied
smirk.

"Hungry?"

The word penetrated her, stabbed her deep as it conjured up images of naked bodies, glistening with sweat and arching against each other, moving in sensual harmony. What would it be like to say yes, to take his hand and lead him back to the guest suite? She'd been a quick study their first time together. Taking control, embracing the emotions coursing through her, delighting in the approval that had glittered in his eyes as his hands had tightened on her hips and guided her up and down...

She closed her eyes for a moment. Savored the memory.

Then released it.

"I've already had breakfast." She nodded toward her plate, empty except for a few bread crumbs and some strawberry leaves. "Also delicious."

It took every ounce of self-control she had not to laugh at his look of consternation as he sat across from her.

"Glad the cooking is at least to your liking," he muttered. He leaned over, snatched a bagel out of the basket a maid had brought out and sat back. She kept her gaze trained on his face and off his chiseled abs.

"Suzie is hosting a final tasting this evening. Appetizers, main course samplers, desserts."

"Hmm."

Irritation nipped any lingering attraction in the bud. "Hmm?"

He took a bite of his bagel. "Mmm-hmm."

She barely stopped herself from slamming her mug on the table as she stood. "Well, I will tell Suzie you agreed to everything with an 'mmm-hmm.'"

"Suzie already knows I agree."

"What?"

He didn't even look at her as he slathered cream cheese on his bagel. "I called her this morning. Nice woman."

She sucked in a slow, deep breath—a better alternative to reaching across the table, grabbing the bagel basket and dumping the contents on his lap. When he did look up, those damned blue eyes were wide and innocent. The devious twinkle and quirked corner of his full lips said he was full of it and up to no good.

As usual.

"You all right, Callie?"

Her obstetrician would probably have had a fit if she could see Calandra's blood pressure right now. She tamped down her rising irritation, at least outwardly, and summoned her iciest smile.

"What did you chat about?"

He bit into the bagel, chewing slowly and leaning farther back in his chair. She silently willed the universe to break one of the chair legs and send him tumbling back onto his arrogant ass.

"We made a few changes to tonight's tasting."

A throbbing started at her temples, low but persistent. "Oh?"

If he heard the warning in her tone, he blazed right past it as he bestowed his most dazzling smile on her. "You'll like them."

"And if I don't?"

"You will."

She laughed. It was that or commit murder with a bagel basket. "Of course. I should have anticipated— what did *Variety* call you? 'Every commitment-minded woman's worst nightmare'—to hire a professional to manage an event that his entire dream rests on and then interfere whenever he feels like it."

He set the bagel down, stood and in three seconds was standing less than a foot away.

"Everyone thinks they know me from those articles." No hint of a smile. His voice was low and dangerous. "Keep in mind, the public sees what I want them to see."

"Ah. So you put on a show?"

"Yes." His eyes narrowed before his gaze dipped down to her lips, then back up. "I'm not the only one in this villa who hides."

The past ripped through her defenses and rendered her speechless. She stared at him, fighting back the retort that she wanted to deliver, that explained why she hid. Hiding had saved her in the past, saved Johanna.

Slowly, she eased herself back into her chair. The irritation slipped from Alejandro's face as he watched her.

"What's wrong?"

She held up a hand, gathering strength before she spoke. Alejandro sat across from her, face serious and eyes searching for answers. She resisted turning away. To do so would only invite more scrutiny. But as she lifted her mug to her lips, she glanced at him from beneath her lashes.

It wasn't just that the depth of her feelings for Alejandro and her lack of control over them terrified the hell out of her, that made her hide and push him away. It wasn't just the possibility of him breaking her heart. It was what would happen to her child when Alejandro left that drove her to keep him at arm's length. She'd had years of being her mother's caregiver to build up her walls, to cocoon herself in apathy and coldness, reserving her emotions only for Mother and Johanna.

It was the one thing that had saved her from suffering the same anguish her mother had when her father had lost interest in her, had abandoned her to living in a lakeside mansion bursting at the seams with everything a little girl could want.

Everything except love.

Love. When Alejandro had helped her in New York, when he'd treated not just her body but *her* with such tenderness, she'd wondered if she'd fallen a little in love. Definitely lust. But his interest in the baby, his dedication to his company…she'd gotten glimpses over the years of the real man he hid away, but she'd never anticipated a leader, a caregiver, a provider.

A lover.

She refocused on her tea. She was not in a position to evaluate him accurately.

"Morning sickness," she finally said as he continued to stare at her.

"Bullshit."

She arched a brow. "You might want to work on that mouth of yours before the baby arrives."

"Don't distract me. It's not just the pregnancy that's bothering you."

A quick shrug of her shoulders. "It's not important."

"It is to me."

Her hands tightened on the mug as her heart swooned. It was scary how much she wanted to believe him, to curl up in his arms and confide every dark event, every secret, surrender to being cared for.

"I appreciate that, Alejandro. I do," she insisted when his eyes narrowed. "However, as kind as that sentiment is, I believe you're using it to distract me from the fact that you messed up my evening."

Her phone buzzed on the table. She picked it up and frowned as she read the text.

Confirming the change of venue for tonight's tasting. Excited to see the yacht!

She had to read it twice before it sank in.

"Your yacht?"

Alejandro frowned. "I wanted to tell you."

"Why?"

"So I could see a glimmer of excitement in those normally staid eyes. That or daggers." He squinted. "Guess I got my wish. If looks could kill—"

"You would have been dead a long time ago." She set her phone and mug on the table and gave in to the desire—no, the need—to massage her temples as the headache grew. "What game are you playing, Alejandro?"

"No game."

"I sincerely doubt that."

The teasing smile disappeared as his lips straightened once more. "Perhaps, instead of assuming I'm playing a game or devising a devious plot, you might instead question how your actions forced me to do this."

Her mouth dropped. "What?"

"This week wasn't supposed to be about work. It was to get to know each other. How is that possible when you're running around Marseille and staying as far away as possible from me?"

The headache unleashed its fury, little pickaxes

hacking away inside her head as she tried to find her footing in the conversation that had seriously spiraled out of control.

"You still had no right to interfere with my work without talking to me first."

"So you could make an excuse?" Brittle laughter tumbled from his lips. "I have no doubt that, had I approached you, you would have tried to find a way around me just like you did when you tried to flee Paris."

"Fleeing is an over exaggeration," she replied coolly. *Calm.* She had to stay calm to maintain the upper hand.

He started to retort, then stopped and pinched the bridge of his nose. "Regardless, the venue has been moved to my yacht. Be ready outside the villa at six."

"Somewhere in that order I heard an invitation."

"Hear what you want." Alejandro stood, his body tense, frustration rolling off him in palpable waves. "So long as you're outside by six."

Perhaps she could accidentally knock him overboard.

"Who will be there?" she asked as he started to turn away.

"You, me, Suzie and whoever she brings. Plus my crew."

The headache faded as warning whispered across the back of her neck. "But...just us? For dinner?"

It was like watching a predator realize it had its prey within its grasp. He leaned forward, hands tightening on the back of the chair as a sensual smile spread across his too-handsome face. "Is that a problem?"

Judging by the electricity that had slowly begun to sizzle in her veins, yes, it was a major problem.

"No. Just curious."

The deepening smile told her he knew better. Knew that right now that heat was pooling between her thighs no matter how sternly she lectured herself to keep it together.

There would be other people on the yacht. But for all intents and purposes, they would be alone.

"Don't think you can seduce me to get what you want."

Alejandro circled the table, muscles rippling as he moved like a panther, swift and confident. Sun gleamed on his bare skin, and she had a frantic recollection of the golden lights from a nearby building creating the same glow on his chest as he'd slid inside her for the first time, big and hard and yet so gentle as the initial discomfort had faded, replaced with a wondrous pleasure that rippled through her with each tender thrust.

"I will get what I want, Calandra," he said as he placed one hand on the table and one on the back of her chair, caging her between his powerful arms. "But not by seduction. When we make love again, it will be because you want me as badly as I want you."

Even she was impressed by her own willpower and ability to keep her face blank. Because if he saw the effect he was having on her, the swirl of heat and need combined with that emotional pull that was so tempting and yet so frightening, she had no doubt he would use it in a heartbeat to make her surrender herself to him. Body and soul.

"Hold on to that fantasy, Alejandro. Because that's the only place you're going to see me naked ever again."

A wolfish smile crossed his face. "We'll see."

Before she could pull back, he leaned down…and

placed a kiss on her forehead. She should have pushed him away, far away, instead of closing her eyes and, for one brief, reckless moment, allowing herself to just *feel*.

And then he straightened.

"Six tonight. Don't be late."

And then he was gone, leaving her with the sinking feeling that she had just made a colossal mistake.

CHAPTER TWELVE

THE BLACK SHIRT and skirt Calandra wore as she walked down the front steps of the villa only made her look paler. Beautiful, Alejandro acknowledged, but aloof, distant. She walked toward the vintage Rolls-Royce, a purse slung across her body, hair pulled back in a tight braid. If she thought he wouldn't be attracted to her when she dressed like she was going to a funeral, she was dead wrong. The braid bared her face to his gaze, a sight he consumed greedily. Dark brows bringing out her gray eyes, sharp cheekbones offset by that intoxicating, rosebud-shaped mouth.

Beautiful. He knew how to work with beautiful. But as she drew closer, her hand straying to the tiny bump beneath her shirt, he knew a moment of uncertainty. The women he'd known before had been easy to deal with and, most of the time, fun. For some, he'd been a shoulder to lean on. For others, he'd been a body to enjoy as they pushed memories of past lovers out of their mind. For a select few who had not heeded his caution that he was only interested in a good time, he'd been the target of angry tears and smeared mascara as they'd thrown shoes, hairbrushes or, in the case of a beautiful symphony percussionist with a passionate temper, a glockenspiel.

But this…this was new territory. Not just because she carried his child inside her. She fought him at every turn, resisted his usually successful charms and scorned the wealth that previous women of his acquaintance fawned over.

She fascinated him.

He glanced down at his watch, not ready to have her see how much she affected him beyond the physical attraction. "Five fifty-nine. I'm impressed."

Her eyes flickered over him, her gaze opaque.

"I'm impressed you're wearing clothes."

He cracked a grin. "Figured I'd try something new since my state of undress doesn't seem to affect you."

"Fishing for compliments, are we?"

"I'm not above begging."

She stopped in front of him. The faintest scent of sandalwood mixed with something surprisingly soft and fruity—cherries?—teased him. He resisted the urge to lean in, inhale her scent and place the faintest of kisses on her lovely neck.

He dragged his gaze from where her pulse beat at the base of her throat up to meet her eyes. Not dark and flinty, but soft and gray.

"You look handsome tonight, Alejandro."

The simple compliment floored him. No over-the-top words, no excessive batting of the eyelashes. Just five words that shot straight into his chest.

He opened the door and gave her an exaggerated bow. "It's a start. After you, mademoiselle."

How big of a bastard was he that he was encouraging her to open up to him while throwing up his own defenses? His conscience bugged him the entire ride into Marseille as he regaled her with the history of the town and pointed out various landmarks.

They arrived at the harbor, and he escorted her onto the teakwood deck of the yacht.

"*Bonjour*, Mademoiselle Smythe!" Suzie said happily as Calandra walked onboard. "I am so excited for this opportunity."

"Thank you for changing your plans so quickly."

He ignored Calandra's barb and, with a quick murmur of thanks to Suzie, guided Calandra in the direction of the stairs.

"Al fresco dining on the sundeck as we cruise around the Gulf. Suzie and her team will cater, and we'll have some privacy."

She tossed him her signature raised brow. "I'm not having sex with you on the deck of your yacht."

"Ah. Well, since you figured out my sneaky plan, should we just cancel the tasting and go back to the villa?"

A roll of the eyes, but she didn't turn quickly enough to hide the smile that quirked her lips.

They reached the deck, and he had the pleasure of seeing her eyes widen as she took in the splendor of *La Pimpinela Escarlata*. Plush couches were arranged around a small fire pit filled with glittering glass. Beyond the couches, a crystal-clear pool glimmered beneath the lights of the port and the emerging moon. And on the far side of the sundeck, two red velvet chairs and a white table decked with votive candles and set for two.

He turned to Calandra, waiting for her compliments on the custom wood decking, the hand-stitched silk pillows or any of the other details former lovers had gushed over when he'd brought them here.

Nothing. Nothing but that analytical stare sweeping over everything.

"It's nice," she finally said.

He bit down on his own tongue as he clasped her elbow and walked across the sundeck toward the table.

"Glad it's satisfactory."

If she sensed the irritation in his voice, she didn't acknowledge it. She sat down, crossed her legs and watched the buildings of Marseille grow smaller as the yacht pulled away from the port.

Suzie bustled over to the table and set two plates in front of them with a flourish.

"Monsieur Cabrera, Mademoiselle Smythe told me of your appreciation for old-world glamour."

He glanced at Calandra, who was examining the food on her plate with a critical eye.

"Yes. *La Reina*'s renovation was inspired by cruises from an earlier generation. My mother and I used to watch old movies." A smile tugged at his lips. "One of my favorite memories."

Suzie grinned as Calandra looked up, her gaze searching. He'd never shared that tidbit before. A small fact, so why did he feel bare, like he'd just revealed something deep?

"That makes me happy to hear. Like *Gentlemen Prefer Blondes*, yes? Or *An Affair to Remember*?"

Hearing the familiar names brought on a rush of nostalgia. "Two of my mother's favorites, actually."

"Good." Suzie gestured to the plate in front of him. "I also share an affinity for such films. For your tasting tonight, you have oysters Rockefeller, baked in a butter sauce, *socca* flatbread with a salmon tartare and baked camembert with honey and red pepper. And for you," she said, turning to Calandra, "I have prepared a traditional French dish, coquilles St. Jacques, seared scallops on cucumber slices. And then brie fondant au pesto, topped with pine nuts and served with grapes and toasted baguette slices." She put her hands on her hips and beamed. "A mix of your old-world glamour and French favorites."

As much as he'd balked at the idea of a culinary school catering the party that could make or break his company, he found himself eyeing the food with appreciation. Not only did it smell incredible, but the delicate touches, from the sprinkling of chives over the scallops to the lemon wedges arranged artfully around the oysters, lent an artistic flair.

"This looks wonderful," Calandra said. The smile she bestowed on Suzie had him blinking in shock. Sweet, feminine, kind. He realized with a jolt that he was now privy to one of the reasons why Calandra had been so successful in her job with Cabrera Wines. She hid her warm and fuzzy side well. But when she pulled it out of wherever she'd been hiding it, she dazzled.

"My students were very excited at the prospect of cooking for a famous billionaire, not to mention on his personal yacht." Suzie beamed. "But we shall see what you think of the food. Eat!"

And with that pronouncement, she left. The yacht cut across the water, the brilliant sapphire of the sky stretching down to meet the darker blue of the ocean. The bell tower and stone walls of the Notre-Dame de la Garde stood proudly on a hill overlooking Marseille as the port grew smaller on the horizon.

"It is beautiful."

Alejandro glanced at Calandra. With her face turned toward Marseille, her pale profile stood out in stark, stunning contrast against the sky.

"How much did it cost you to admit that?"

Instead of her customary silence or a sharp retort, she surprised him with a small smile that twisted his stomach into a tight knot.

"It's too beautiful not to acknowledge."

Before he could say anything else, he picked up a scallop and cucumber slice and popped it into her mouth. Her eyes widened.

"Oh, my."

Her moan of pleasure made his blood boil. Pushing past his lust, he scooped up a piece of baked camembert with the flatbread, then sat back in surprise as the sweetness of honey and spice of red pepper hit his tongue.

"Well?"

"Decent."

"Decent?" she repeated. "This is wonderful and you know it."

He shrugged and took a sip of water, enjoying stretching out the moment. "Better than some places I've eaten."

She started to retort, but then her eyes narrowed. "You're teasing me."

"I would never."

She scooped a generous helping of brie and pine nuts onto a baguette slice and held it out. "Try this."

He leaned forward and, before she could snatch her hand away, bit into the bread. Her eyes widened as she sucked in a breath. Her hand trembled. He reached out and caught her wrist before she dropped the baguette. Beneath his fingertips, her pulse pounded so furiously it echoed in his head.

"Delicious."

Her cheeks flamed pink. No, not immune to him at all.

Food first. Then, perhaps later, he could offer her a private tour of the master suite. Optimism and lust had directed his instructions to the staff to make the king-size bed up with black silk sheets and a red rose on the pillow just in case the tide really turned in his favor.

Suzie distracted him from his lascivious thoughts with the next course. Over the next hour she kept up a steady delivery of culinary treasures. In between bites, Alejandro peppered Calandra with questions about her life back in Kitty Hawk, her time in college, the internship that had led her to Cabrera Wines. She, in turn, surprised him by asking not about business, but his movie marathons with his mother, his years at university and his time as a deckhand. His story of nearly getting swept overboard during a nasty storm on the Atlantic elicited more reaction than the luxury surrounding her.

"I don't think most heads of corporations would do that."

"It was fun. I actually enjoyed it. I earned the respect of my crew. When I presented everything I wanted to change to the board, they liked what I had to say."

"And your father?"

The relaxation that had settled in vanished at the mention of his sire.

"My father pointed out Adrian's sales of Cabrera

Wines and told me once I hit that level of profit, then he would congratulate me."

She stabbed her fork into the salmon sitting atop a pile of creamy risotto. "I may not approve of all aspects of your lifestyle, but that's just cruel to do to your son, let alone someone who accomplished so much in such a short time."

Her defense of him was surprisingly touching. When had anyone paid attention to him? Just him?

He couldn't really recall.

After the last course was served, Suzie's students replaced the table and chairs with the lounge chaises that normally occupied that spot. Calandra sat down and stretched out, her face content as the sun sank behind the waves of the Mediterranean, leaving behind fingers of pink and orange clinging to the sky as stars started to twinkle, little pinwheels of light against the darkening sky.

"You were right."

She glanced up at him. "Oh?"

"Some of the best food I've ever had."

Another smile that kicked him hard. "I'm glad you liked it. If the board wasn't already planning to vote yes, they'll have to after a meal like that."

Her belief in his plan touched him in a way he didn't care to examine too closely. At least not now. He shrugged. "Hopefully."

Her eyes latched onto him, gray and pensive and searching. "I've noticed when you shrug, it means you care about something."

"Come again?"

"When you shrug, others see a casual, fly-by-the-seat-of-his-pants, spoiled billionaire. Nothing fazes you." She tilted her head. "I think it's how you hide."

"Hide?" he echoed as he sat down on the lounge next to her.

"You're more than just a playboy, Alejandro." Her unexpected words made him pause. Was her view of him changing? "If your board knows anything about business, they'll know that voting yes on *La Reina* is the best thing to do. You have a solid business plan, and more importantly, you believe in it." Her eyes stayed trained on his, and, God help him, he couldn't look away. "You're more than most people think you are. I have no idea why you act otherwise."

Because I don't know any other way.

Suddenly, the possibility of altering her perceptions, of showing her the man he was just coming to know himself, made him extremely uncomfortable. The few times he'd opened that door with Javier, the rejections had cut deeper and deeper until he'd locked the door and thrown away the key.

"Perhaps it's not an act."

He sensed her disappointment with his answer but steeled himself against saying anything else. His campaign to woo Calandra had been based on wowing her with his wealth and showing her that he didn't spend every waking hour drinking and smoking cigars. He hadn't anticipated this deep dive into emotions that were better left untouched.

"How long until we're back in port?" she asked.

His lips parted. What would she say if he told her everything?

Fear snatched his confession away, leaving him hollow and cold. He glanced at the passing rocky cliffs of Calanques National Park.

"Less than an hour."

She pulled a notebook out of her purse. "In that case, I did have some details I wanted to verify for the party—"

"Don't you ever take a break?"

She looked up at him in surprise.

"When there's time, yes."

"It's after eight o'clock. Nighttime," he added.

"I'm not surprised that you view this as a time to…relax or enjoy." She kept her eyes trained on her damned list. "But not all of us have the luxury of drinking and seducing our way through the evening."

The frosty tone rankled him. Even if he hadn't confessed all, he'd let her see more of *him*, whoever he was, than he'd ever shared with another woman. Because he hadn't responded the way she wanted, she'd resorted to jabs that once would have made him laugh, but now just made his teeth grind.

"All right." He leaned back against the chaise and closed his eyes.

"All right?"

"Mmm-hmm."

"Was there something else you wanted to discuss?"

"Just persuading you to let me be involved in my child's life."

For a moment there was only the distant sound of the ocean waves.

"When you say it like that, it sounds awful," she said.

Irritation flared into anger. He opened his eyes,

swung his legs over so his feet rested on the deck and faced her, letting her see the depth of his displeasure.

"It is awful, Calandra. You're threatening to not let me be involved in my own child's life."

"That's not what I said. I just—"

"'Birthday parties and such,'" he quoted back at her. "Isn't that what you said in Paris?"

"I didn't mean you couldn't ever see the baby, I just…"

"Just what?" When she continued to stare at him, her face blank, he barely stopped himself from grabbing her shoulders. "Just be involved when you say it's allowed? Maybe that's once a year, maybe once every three years?"

She came to life, exploding with passion and energy as she leaned forward, eyes blazing.

"Fine, then! Take me to court, sue me for custody or whatever it is you want. God knows you have enough money to get whatever you want."

"What I want," he ground out, trying to figure out how this conversation had spiraled so quickly out of control, "is not to force the mother of my child into doing something she doesn't want to do. Yes, I slept with dozens of women. I swung from the chandelier at the Venetian Hotel. I've spent money on God knows what. But I've always tried to do right by the people in my life, and that includes you. Why are you so afraid of me?"

"I'm not afraid of you!"

He leaned in then, his lips just a breath away from hers. Her breathing stopped, then resumed with a deep, shuddering inhale.

"Perhaps you should be, Calandra." Just a touch

closer. "Perhaps I make you feel things that frighten you. Things you want but for whatever reason won't let yourself have."

She swallowed hard. "I'm not going to make the same mistake my mother did."

As she started to stand, the deck tilted. A small movement from the lapping of the waves, but enough of a surprise that it threw Calandra off balance. He stood and caught her.

And then she was in his arms and he didn't know whether it was the roaring of the ocean or the blood thundering in his ears. All he knew was that her hands still lay on his chest, his arms were still wrapped around her waist. They stared at each other, waiting.

Just when he thought he wouldn't be able to contain himself any longer, her arms wrapped around his neck and she pressed her lips flush against his.

CHAPTER THIRTEEN

HE BURST INTO FLAMES. His body hardened everywhere as he crushed her against him, running his tongue along the seam of her lips, demanding entry. She gasped, opened beneath him, moaning as he tasted her.

Their lips fused together as he sat down on the chaise, stretched out with her body clutched against his. His hand slid under her shirt. Her mouth opened on a gasp as he cupped her swollen breast. He teased her by tracing his tongue over her lips as his fingers plucked at her nipple.

Until she nearly undid him by grabbing the back of his head and crushing his lips to hers, slipping her own tongue inside in a brazen, seductive move that made him so hard it almost hurt.

Dios, she was incredible. Fiery, strong, fearless. He couldn't get enough of her, needed more. He pulled her shirt up, the cup of her bra down and sucked her nipple into his mouth.

"Alejandro!"

A tiny thread of sanity pushed through, whispering that they could be discovered at any moment. But he didn't care. This was his yacht and she was *his*. His, and he couldn't have stopped touching her even if he wanted to.

He reached down as he continued to kiss and suck her breasts, bunched up the material of her skirt until his fingertips met the bare skin of her thigh. She arched against him and—*querido Dios*—he could feel the heat of her core against his erection straining against his jeans.

"Alejandro…"

Hearing her name tumble from his lips drove him mad. He tore his mouth from her breast, trailed kisses over her cheek and down her neck. With a quick yank, her skirt ended up around her waist and he peeled away her panties.

Her red, lacy panties that made him so hot with desire it was all he could do to keep himself from stripping them both naked and making love to her right then and there on the sundeck.

"I just…they're not…" She stumbled over her words, withdrawing into herself. "I don't—"

He tucked the panties into his pocket, rolled and laid her beneath him. Then he pulled her skirt up and placed his mouth on her. She arched, thrusting her hips against him as he tasted her sweetness.

"Alejandro!"

She was liquid fire in his arms. Stripped bare of not just the unexpected lingerie but all her defenses. He looked up, caught her gaze in his and watched as her eyes flamed molten silver as his tongue danced over her most sensitive skin. Knowing that he had been her first, that he was her only, made his fingers tighten on her thighs as he upped his sensual assault. A maddening urge drove him onward as he used the cues of her body—the hitch in her breathing, the clench of her thighs, the arch of her back—to guide his lovemaking and ensure she never even entertained the thought of sharing her body with another man.

Just the idea of another man touching her, let alone engaging in this kind of intimacy, made him see red. Jealousy like he'd never known before shot through his veins and he buried his face between her legs, savored the sound of her crying out his name.

Mine, mine, mine, an inner beast roared.

Her fingers tangled in his hair. He paused. He hadn't planned on ravishing her like this, of being brought to the edge of his control. It would be a very long night, but if she wanted him to stop, he would.

And then her fingers tightened and she spread her thighs even more with a whispered "Please" that made his blood boil. He licked her, kissed, nibbled, experimented with what made her whimper, what made her gasp, what made her demand more.

Her thighs clenched. Her breathing grew more frantic, her hips thrusting harder. He buried his tongue inside her as he envisioned what it would be like to finally sheath himself inside her tight wetness again.

She exploded, writhing against the chaise as he kissed her most vulnerable spot, made love to her with his tongue until she collapsed, body shuddering, fingers still tangled in his hair but limp.

He stretched out next to her, tugging her skirt back into place as he cradled her body against his. She leaned into his embrace, her head resting on his shoulder.

Something sparked inside him. Not just the lust that was roaring through his veins, not the desire that was tightening his chest until he thought he would explode if he couldn't feel her luscious body wrapped around him.

No, this was something else. A protectiveness, a need to not only claim her body with his own but to keep her safe. To wipe away whatever pain had fueled the defenses she normally kept in place with icy precision.

Slowly, she raised her head. Her eyes glowed silver under the light of the stars. Luminous, bright with satisfaction and…

Fear. He saw the fear flickering deep in the gray depths, felt her uncertainty as her hands rested on his shoulders.

"Calandra, what just happened—"

"Can't happen again."

Her words stopped him cold. "What?"

It almost hurt to watch the change that came over her. The coldness that eclipsed the lingering passion in her eyes. The straightening of her shoulders as she pulled away from him. The firming of her lips as she stood, smoothed her skirt and sat down on the other chaise.

That a woman could box him up and push away so neatly after such a heated, passionate encounter—in the middle of the damned ocean—and then react with all the cool efficiency of a military general rubbed him raw.

That that woman was also carrying his child made the wound especially grievous.

"I'm sorry, Alejandro. I kissed you first and started our…that is—"

"Our lovemaking?"

He hadn't thought it possible, but her face grew harder.

"Don't call it that."

If he hadn't just held her in his arms, felt her come apart beneath his lips, he would never have thought the ice queen sitting before him capable of the passion she'd just displayed.

But she had. Others might confuse this withdrawal for her being rude, or even a "stone-cold bitch," as he'd heard one waiter snap at an event when Calandra had taken him to task for showing up late in wrinkled clothing. Was he the only one who had glimpsed her pain? The only one who had seen her staunch loyalty to those she believed in, like Suzie and her culinary students?

"What would you like me to call it?"

"A mistake."

It wasn't just his pride that she hurt. No, those two words crawled beneath his skin and lodged somewhere near his heart, seeping into his body with a black, poisonous pain that made him question himself.

Not enough. He'd wondered over the years what it would be like to surrender his playboy image, to settle into a relationship. Most marriages in his world were power plays. But that hadn't stopped the curiosity, nor the loneliness that sometimes invaded after he left yet another bed at the crack of dawn. A hell of his own making, but one that had grown tiresome.

Yet he'd never wanted to risk trying. Who was he without his money, his power, his reputation? The women who had expected more from him hadn't wanted *him.* They'd wanted his lifestyle, possessions, notoriety.

Until Calandra. The woman who had given herself

to him, then turned around and presented him with yet another gift. Who made him want more, to be more.

And then crushed him before he could even try.

He smiled, the distant smile he'd perfected over the years. She blinked, some of the glacial condemnation slipping from her face.

"Alejandro, I—"

"You're absolutely right." He nodded at the lights of Marseille on the horizon. "I might enjoy seducing women all over the world, but on the deck of a ship when we could have been caught was crass to say the least."

She started to reach out, to settle her fingers on his arm, but he stood and stepped out of reach.

"I hope this incident hasn't ruined my chances of being involved with our child."

She shook her head. Her eyes gleamed, and for a moment his commitment wavered. Were those tears?

Doesn't matter.

"No. And I'm sorry, Alejandro."

He bowed his head before she could say anything else. "Me, too. I took advantage of you."

"No!"

"Yes. It won't happen again." He turned and walked away. She'd done it to him twice now. Once in New York, and once on the deck of his own yacht.

It probably made him cruel, no better than his father. But he couldn't stop the grim satisfaction that settled in his bones as his footsteps carried him farther away from the one woman who he had realized, too late, held too much power over him.

A positive of his facade. When he hurt, when he felt too much, he could pull the mantle of his pretense around him like a shield and distract himself with the vices he'd indulged in over the years.

For tonight, at least, the vices would keep the heart-wrenching pain at bay.

CHAPTER FOURTEEN

THE WAVES OF the Mediterranean were sharper this morning, capped white as a brisk wind barreled over the water. Clouds darkened the horizon, puffy gray transitioning to a dark slate that advanced ever closer toward land.

Memories assailed her, of another stormy day long ago when rain had fallen into Lake Geneva as she sat on the window seat of her mother's room. Johanna and she had escaped into the luxury of their mother's suite as thunder had roared. Mom had been in bed, her skin so papery thin Calandra had imagined she could see her bones just below the surface.

Johanna had climbed into bed and snuggled against Mom's listless body. Calandra, unable to stomach the knowledge that their mother was wasting away from a broken heart, had gone to the window seat, leaned her head against the cold glass and watched the drops fall onto the lake.

"Calandra," her mother had whispered at last. Calandra had turned to look back at her, dark hair spread across the pillow, lips pale so that when she smiled, she looked like a ghost.

And then she'd uttered the words that had governed Calandra's life ever since.

You're so strong.

Was it the weather taking her to such dark memories? Or her own cringeworthy actions from the night before? She'd relived seeing that smile on his face, that horrid smile that she had put there with her cold words and her casual dismissal of the passion they'd shared, at least a dozen times since she'd gotten up.

It hadn't been his fault. Far from it. *She* had been the one to kiss *him*. Once she started, she hadn't been able to stop, her desire an addiction she'd needed to sate.

And then she'd been so angry with herself, so horrified at her behavior, that she'd taken it out on him.

Alejandro had called a driver to pick her up at the port and take her back to the villa. After spending an hour crafting half a dozen statements as she'd paced the guest quarters, she'd tossed them all out the window and decided that maybe, just for once, she'd wing it, let her emotions and remorse speak for themselves when Alejandro returned.

But he hadn't come back. She'd sat up until nearly one in the morning waiting for his headlights to appear on the drive. Doubt had crept in with every passing of the hand on the clock in her room. She'd found her release under his skillful lovemaking. He'd had none. What if he had decided to seek out someone in Marseille? It wouldn't be any of her business; they weren't a couple, and her treatment of him—her employer, the father of her child, her only lover to date—had been abhorrent.

She had absolutely no business being jealous. No reason for experiencing the same kind of hurt she'd felt when she'd spotted that tabloid magazine at the supermarket and seen him walking into the hotel in London with that actress on his arm, gazing up at him in adoration.

At least that's what she kept telling herself as she sipped her tea.

Thunder rumbled across the water, soft yet so deep she felt it in her bones. The sensation relaxed her muscles as she leaned back into her chair.

An angry voice yanked away her precious moment of peace. She sat straight up, her head whipping around as furious Spanish filled the air.

Calandra's breath caught when she caught full sight of him. His hair was combed back from his face, damp like he'd just come out of the shower. With a loose gray shirt hanging off his broad shoulders, blue jeans clinging to those muscular legs and bare feet padding against the patio stones, the sexily casual look fanned the lust that seemed to always be within arm's reach these days.

It wasn't just how perfectly his clothes molded to his physique, though. No, it was the firmness in his granite jaw, the blazing anger in his stormy eyes, the tautness of his biceps beneath the shirtsleeves as he cursed into the phone.

"Terminamos con esta conversación. Adiós."

He dropped into the chair opposite her. He blinked, then suddenly focused on her as if seeing her for the first time. The anger disappeared as he flashed her a cocky grin. One that didn't quite reach his eyes.

"Parents. Hopefully I do better in that role than my father."

He said it in jest, but his words caught her attention. "He wasn't a good father?"

It was like watching a door being slammed shut as his face hardened. Just as it had last night. He grabbed an orange from the fruit bowl and focused his attention on peeling it.

"Room for improvement. How are you feeling this morning?"

A deft change of subject. But she followed his lead.

"Good." She sucked in a breath. Time to apologize. Except the words froze in her throat as he bit into an orange slice. Juice dribbled down his chin. He swiped a hand across his chin and sucked the juice off a finger. Her heartbeat kicked into overdrive, remembering the way he'd sucked her nipple into his mouth last night as his hands had drifted...

"Calandra?"

"Sorry." She mentally shook her head as she met his amused gaze. The bastard knew exactly what she'd been thinking. "What did you say?"

"I told the crew about the change in caterers. They're excited to have Suzie and her crew."

When the words registered, a thrill shot through her. "Really?"

"Yes. The food was spectacular, the service impeccable." He shrugged. "Wasn't expecting it, but they did well. And supporting a local school will bring in good publicity and earn us some points with the community."

She didn't even bother hiding her satisfied smile. "Thank you."

He cocked his head, his eyes narrowed as he assessed her for a moment. "It's I who should be thanking you." His bark of laughter was harsh. "Well, that and that I'm the one making the decisions regarding this event. Javier told me I was ruining my chances at swaying the board before I even started."

"Is that what you were arguing about?"

"That and you. Not about…" He gestured toward her stomach with the half-eaten orange. "That."

"That?"

"What am I supposed to call it? We don't know if it's a boy or a girl."

"The baby?"

Alejandro rolled his eyes. "That's so…plain."

The conversation was so…normal, she realized with a start. As if they were an ordinary couple bickering good-naturedly over finding out the sex of their child. It stirred a longing for other normal things, like having a partner to share that first smile with.

"Anyway," Alejandro continued, unaware of her inner turmoil, "I told him I hired you to oversee the last details. He already thinks I'm wasting time and money on this venture as it is."

"I imagine your half-a-million-dollar payout for one week didn't sit well."

"None of his business. Yes, I'm paying you more because I impregnated you." He held up a hand as she opened her mouth to retort. "But I'm also paying you what you're worth. You earned an MBA from MIT and you worked for Cabrera Wines for three years. That's after your four-year stint at another firm as an associate event planner."

The retort died as she sat back, stunned. "You know all that about me?"

"Yes." He held her gaze for a long moment. "I didn't just stare at your cleavage at those events."

She arched a brow. "You looked at my ass, too?"

"It's a great ass." A grin flashed, then was unexpectedly replaced by a serious countenance. "But I listened, too. I know you increased Cabrera Wines' event attendance by two hundred percent over two years. I know you got Adrian that feature in *Time* because they heard about his parties. I'm paying you what you're worth, Calandra."

Other than Aunt Norine, no one had ever stood up for her. She'd learned early and she'd learned hard. She had no one to depend on but herself.

Until now. Even when she'd found out about the baby, every time she'd envisioned the future, it had been with Johanna those first couple of years, then alone as Johanna moved on with her life. Just her and her child. But every time Alejandro did something like this, the image of a family became more vivid, more enticing.

That he'd still defend her after last night meant even more. It also laid bare a truth she could no longer deny—he had hired her for *her*. Unlike Father, who'd used money to manipulate situations and people to his advantage, Alejandro believed in her.

Seconds ticked by. Calandra kept her eyes trained on the ocean, the rise and fall of the turquoise waves, and off Alejandro.

She could feel him, though. Watching her. That gaze, the color of the sea, laying waste to the wall she'd built over the years and stripping her bare until she felt naked. Exposed.

"Your father is a fool," she finally said. A fool for doubting his son, for trying to micromanage a brilliant mind. For whatever he'd done to hurt his son.

Alejandro ran a hand through his hair, dark curls pulled back to reveal the sharpness of his cheekbones, the strong cut of his jaw, before falling back down to graze the tanned column of his neck.

"He is. But I spent years acting like a fool just to try to piss him off." His teeth flashed white in the morning sunlight. "Although I've been quite successful."

She shook her head, trying and failing to suppress a smile. "You do excel at pissing people off."

Alejandro's grin disappeared as he glanced down to where her hand still lay protectively over the slight swell of her stomach.

Calandra's nose wrinkled. "When will you tell him?"

"I don't know. I doubt he'll be excited by his greatest disappointment siring offspring. But don't worry," he added with a reassuring smile. "The rest of the family will be more supportive. And kind. Especially my mother. She'll be thrilled."

His words sliced through the camaraderie and brought her crashing back to reality. Since the age of twelve, it had been her, Johanna and Aunt Norine. And Aunt Norine had been gone for almost two years now.

Just the thought of Alejandro being involved had been hard to digest. Toss in his mother, two billionaire brothers, a fiancée and a bastard of a father, and she could barely keep her tea down.

But that was for another time. She paused. He'd been the one to initiate their encounters so far. As he'd pointed out, if they were truly going to get to know each other better, they needed to spend time together.

"I have a few details to confirm for the party, but if the storm passes, I thought about going to Calanques

National Park this afternoon." She inhaled deeply. "Would you like to join me?"

He blinked. Time passed, each second stretching longer than the last. Another rumble of thunder rolled across the landscape, louder and more aggressive as the amber liquid in her teacup trembled.

"Unfortunately," Alejandro finally said, "I have a virtual meeting with my father most of the day and tomorrow to discuss the construction delays and review finances."

His rejection sliced through her. No animosity in his words, no cruelty on his face. But she had no doubt that, had she not let her fear get the better of her last night, he would have been interested, perhaps even excited, to spend time with her.

"I hope it goes well," she managed to force out.

He stood and bowed his head to her and started to walk off, head held high, his stride steady. Something, though, was amiss. It should frighten her, how easily she was able to pick up on his moods now, discern that something was wrong.

"Alejandro."

He turned and glanced back at her.

"I'm sorry. About last night." She looked down at her hands. "I took out my own insecurities on you."

A shrug. "Happens. I could have handled it better."

She swallowed hard. He was accepting her apology. Time to let it go.

"Thank you. And…" She floundered for a moment, trying to find the right words. "I know how much the renovation of *La Reina* means to you. I thought hiring me was just a way to give me money. Even though I think you're still overpaying me—" his lips quirked "—I know it wasn't just that."

He nodded. "You're welcome."

And then he left. Still the confident walk, back straight, head tall. Yet something dark seemed to cling to his shoulders, slow his stride as he walked away and didn't look back.

Leaving her alone with the encroaching thunder, the dark swirl of the sea and her own storm of emotions waging war inside her chest.

CHAPTER FIFTEEN

ALEJANDRO KNOCKED ON Calandra's door. He'd closed the laptop on his meeting in the library and come straight to the guest suite. Over the last eleven hours, eight of them had been spent poring over records and reports or engaging in heated arguments with his sire.

If he wasn't exhausted, he would question why his first thought had been to come see Calandra. However, since he could barely keep his eyes open, he didn't care to examine his reasoning. He just wanted to see her. Her offer of time together had been an olive branch, one that had surprised him after last night's acrimonious parting. Pride had inspired his refusal. Pain had flared in her eyes, spurring his flight from the patio.

Coward.

This time, he didn't shove the thought aside. He'd labeled his previous departures from uncomfortable situations as spur-of-the-moment, a distaste for conflict or, in the case of his father, survival.

But the more he thought about it, the more he realized those had just been excuses. Excuses for running away.

Just like your father.

The thought angered him. He was nothing like his father.

But aren't you? that nasty little voice whispered. Javier had rarely been a part of family functions, from dinners to vacations. But after Alejandro's discovery, he'd been even more absent.

He hadn't been lying about his meetings with Javier. Yet he'd grabbed onto that excuse with both hands. Had seen the hurt flare in her eyes, felt the vulnerable price she'd paid and the pain of rejection in his soul.

The same rejection he'd experienced when she called last night a mistake. The same rejection that, no matter how many successes he'd accumulated, his father still heaped on his shoulders with every criticism of Cabrera Shipping, every snide remark about the women he spent time with—as if the bastard had any room to talk.

The truth of what had happened that morning—that instead of savoring the victory of having Calandra finally offer him what he wanted, he'd run away like a damned *pollo*—had clung to him like a shroud. The stronger the rain had pounded against the window of his office, the blacker his mood had grown. To the point that when Javier had asked in that brisk, holier-than-thou tone if Alejandro would prefer to continue their review at a later date, he hadn't hesitated to say yes.

Javier had blinked, eyes so round with surprise he'd reminded Alejandro of an owl.

"What?"

"I said *sí.*"

"But—"

"We both know you'll make the decisions in the end, Javier, especially if you get your way Saturday night. So," he continued, ignoring his father's gaping mouth, "if you don't mind, I have something more important to deal with."

Slamming the computer screen shut on Javier's face had been gratifying and fortified him for the long trek through the villa to the guest quarters.

And now he stood there, waiting to see which Calandra would open the door. The cold, efficient planner? The passionate lover? Or the vulnerable woman who hid so well behind her wall of ice?

He rubbed the bridge of his nose. A couple days ago, everything had seemed so simple. But he'd been so focused on getting her to see him that he hadn't thought about what getting to know her would do to him. To be reminded not just of their mind-numbing, body-tingling sexual heat, but of the rapport they'd unknowingly developed over the years.

Knowing her better, seeing the woman who cared about supporting a small culinary school and who would fight tooth and nail for her baby, and feeling the urge to share more and more of himself, placed him at a crossroads. He was free-falling into an intoxicating, terrifying emotional tangle he'd never experienced before.

The temptation to go to one of Marseille's lavish clubs, imbibe too many cocktails and leave with some beautiful dancer who would make him forget the last twenty-four hours had been strong last night. But when he thought about actually kissing another woman, touching someone else after what he'd shared with Calandra, he couldn't do it.

He didn't want to seduce just for the sake of physical pleasure. Not anymore. He wanted something more.

If someone were to ask him what, he wouldn't be able to answer. Not yet.

Calandra was at the crux of all this confusion. Maybe more time would not only get him what he wanted in regard to their child, but some answers for this web of feelings he'd become ensnared in.

A shuffling came from behind the door. A moment later a click sounded, and the door swung open.

"Alejandro?"

He didn't even bother trying to hide his stare. In loose linen pants and a seashell-pink tank top, hair unbound and flowing over her shoulders, she looked stunning. The shirt brought out the faintest rosiness in her cheeks. She wore no makeup, no battle paint slashed across her eyelids or bloodred stain on her lips that made women eye her with envy and men with desire and intimidation.

This was Calandra at her rawest. And he couldn't stop looking.

"Is everything all right?" she asked hesitantly.

"You're wearing color."

She glanced down with a frown. "Yes. My usual pants are a little tight. My sister insisted on helping me pack before I flew out and must have snuck them into my suitcase." She tugged at the shirt hem. "The last time I let her do that."

"You look beautiful." Her eyes narrowed, and she opened her mouth. He held up his hand. "Just take the compliment."

She stared at him for a moment, then inclined her head toward him. "Thank you."

He bit back a grin.

"Would you like to take a walk with me?"

She eyed his outstretched hand with uncertainty. "A walk?"

"Yes. You move one foot in front of the other and—"

"Thank you." She shook her head. "You'll fit right in with a child since you have the humor of one."

His heart beat a little faster. After last night, he'd been certain that their heated encounter on the yacht had done anything but convince her he was father material. He'd never been good at waiting, had wanted to press her for an answer, but he didn't. This was by far the most important thing he had ever wanted. It was worth a little patience.

The most important thing?

He pondered that for a moment, held the thought in his hand and weighed being a father against maintaining control over Cabrera Shipping.

Yes.

"Where are we walking to?"

"Just along the beach. The storm has passed and the sun's setting."

Calandra arched a brow. "I thought you were busy with your father?"

"I was. But an entire day with him is more than enough."

Finally, she reached out and took his hand. His fingers closed around hers for the second time in less than twenty-four hours as possession reared its head.

"Shall we?"

He managed to escort her out onto the back patio without dropping a kiss on her bare shoulder. Impressive, given that last night he'd locked himself in his suite with an erection so hard even stroking himself hadn't helped. It had taken a very, very cold shower to cool his ardor.

And even that hadn't stopped him from waking up with his hardness throbbing, muscles taut with desire.

If all he could do right now was hold her hand, then he would do it.

They walked along the beach, the sand still warm from the sun.

"If you're free tomorrow, I've canceled my meeting with him."

Her hand tightened in his. A quick glance at her face revealed nothing.

Then, finally, "I can make some time. Where are we going?"

"Somewhere."

"Somewhere like…?"

"Somewhere like it's a secret."

Her customary roll of the eyes, but this time it was coupled with a small twitch of her lips.

Companionable silence descended, backlit by the ocean waves crashing onto the beach and the damp sand clinging to their bare feet. They circled a bleached hunk of driftwood and headed back toward the house.

"I met your father a couple years ago. I don't recall him coming across as controlling or patronizing."

Alejandro's laughter sounded just like his *padre*'s— sharp and harsh.

"No, he doesn't. He presents one face to the 'genteel world' and another to those he thinks are beneath him. I fall into the latter category."

"What makes you say that?"

Did she see the sudden rise in his chest as he

breathed in deeply, trying to control the anger that was never far out of reach when he thought about Javier?

"He's been breathing down my neck since I took over Cabrera Shipping. Every time I've brought up *La Reina*, he points out every possible scenario where the whole plan falls apart. Never anything that could go right."

Calandra frowned. "Perhaps he's worried about you."

This time his laughter rang out down the beach, startling a couple of seagulls who squawked in indignation and took flight.

"My father doesn't get worried about me. He gets worried about three things—my mother, business and if I'm going to do something to embarrass him."

Her frown deepened. "Have you embarrassed him often?"

"Oh, all the time," he responded cheerfully. "It became a bit of a game in my Eton days. How far could I push him until he snapped."

"Oh."

The way she said it made it sound as if she'd just had a revelation.

"Oh?"

"Sometimes I see a different side of you. This morning when you stood up to your father. Yesterday with Suzie. That night in New York…"

"That night in New York?" His casual tone belied his erection hardening once more, so heavy the cloth of his jeans rubbed against his hot skin. "Hmm…not coming to mind. Perhaps you can describe it for me. In lurid detail, please. My mind's a bit fuzzy."

"If I did describe it, I imagine you wouldn't be able to finish our walk," she said dryly.

"Touché. By the way…" He leaned in, savored the flare of heat in her gaze. "If we ever make love again, it'll be because you initiated."

Her eyes narrowed. "I did last night."

The pert response, delivered with such class, made him grin.

"I want you." He leaned in closer still. There would be no doubt in her mind that he wanted her. "But I'm not going to jeopardize my future with our child by overstepping."

As soon as she made that first move, he would take up the reins and show her everything one night of sex and a hot session of foreplay hadn't afforded them.

"Now that that's established, back to your fascinating psychological profile of my father."

She glanced at him from beneath her lashes. Would she choose now to challenge him?

"I just wonder if, deep down, your father responds like that because he's worried about you. Worried you'll get caught by some gold digger."

Nothing like talking about his father to cool his libido. "Not his style." The cavalier response covered a bone-deep hurt, that of a young boy whose father had no time for him as he traveled the world.

They reached the stone path leading back up to the villa. Electric lanterns lit the walk, casting a romantic glow over the landscape.

"I pulled out the file I've been keeping on *La Reina*, some of the old ships that inspired her renovation." He nodded toward the floor-to-ceiling windows of his office, glinting in the light from the setting sun. "I can show them to you."

"I'd like that. I got a good impression when I toured, but more information is always better."

Pride straightened his shoulders. He'd shown the plans to plenty of people, some who had appreciated, some who had seen dollar signs and some who had seen nothing but an old ship. Sharing the plans with someone who would not only see the business possibilities but the motivation, the inspiration, made him feel as excited as a child showing off their first school drawing.

They walked across the lawn and up the stairs to the glass doors that led into his office. Calandra stopped in the doorway as he flicked on the lights.

"What?"

She surveyed the room for a moment, narrowed eyes darting back and forth. "Just looking."

He turned and looked over the cathedral-size room, trying to see it through her eyes. Sleek gold-and-white office furniture sat atop a shiny, black marble floor. A modern white desk was positioned in one corner, the black executive chair facing the bank of windows that looked out over the backyard.

The first time his father had set foot in this office, it had done exactly what it was supposed to do—made him grimace and shift uncomfortably in the chair placed in the middle of the room, directly across from Alejandro's desk. A trick he'd learned from Adrian's office in Granada.

But now, as Calandra walked through, her eagle eyes missing nothing, something shifted. Something uncomfortable. She saw the office for what it was.

Something he'd picked because it was what people expected, not because it was what he wanted.

Her eyes landed on the one untidy space in the room—the mound of paperwork spread across the desk.

"What's all this?"

"Research. If the worst should happen, at least I'll go down fighting. Use the money I have saved up to make a go of *La Reina* on my own."

Her gray eyes fixed on him.

"I stand by what I said."

He arched a brow. "Which part?"

She gestured to the stack of papers. "I knew you were in charge of Cabrera Shipping. But I didn't realize you took such an active interest in the company."

"Thought I just drank and smoked cigars and laid about with models while much lesser paid men took care of the real work?"

Her blush reappeared, but she didn't blink. "Yes."

"I do. Did," he amended. "Not as much the past year."

"Why?"

"Cabrera Shipping took up more of my time." He glanced down at the two-dimensional rendering of *La Reina*'s top deck, his fingers tracing the lines with pride. "The company has always been the one thing I felt tied to. But it was still given to me by my father. I didn't earn it." Bitterness warred with the discomfort of knowing his increasingly outrageous antics in college had not given Javier any incentive to bestow one of his more lucrative holdings upon his middle son. "At the time I inherited it, I hadn't done much with my life. The company was not in good shape. My father probably thought it was a safe bet to give me because they were already planning for it to die."

"And then you did the impossible."

It was ridiculous how much warmth her words triggered.

"I did. Ruined my father's expectations again," he added with a cheerful note that belied the pain of rejection that still stung so many years later, "just in a different way. But *La Reina* is the first thing that's truly mine. Well, that and…" He nodded toward her stomach. "Two things now. So long as I didn't make too big of a mistake last night."

She flinched, and he inwardly cursed.

"I wasn't trying to make you feel bad, Calandra, just—"

She held up a hand. "Don't. I said it this morning, but I'll say it again. I'm so very sorry, Alejandro, for the way I treated you last night. I was embarrassed by my own behavior and I took it out on you."

He risked a step in her direction. "Why?"

"Because I've never acted like that. And I…" Her voice trailed off, grew quiet. "I don't want to make the same mistakes."

"The same mistakes as your mother?"

She moved over to a window and looked out over the ocean, the waves capped with the oranges and reds of the setting sun, her back to him. Her hair tumbled uncharacteristically down her back, but her neck was straight as a board, shoulders thrust back proudly.

But now he knew to look for the other signs. The tension tightening her muscles, arms wrapped around her waist. Funny how he'd always thought of those gestures as cold, a lack of interest in people or relationships. He knew better now, the depth of emotion she was capable of, the relationships she could build with people like Suzie in a matter of hours.

"My father…" She paused and inhaled deeply. "My father was very wealthy. Not quite Cabrera level of wealth, but wealthy enough that we had a house on Lake Geneva."

Alejandro's eyebrows shot up. "Oh?"

Her gaze stayed trained on the landscape outside, but he noted the slight tightening of her arms, as if she were hugging herself tighter. An ache built in his chest and he almost stepped forward, to pull her back against his chest and cradle her, to make her feel safe as she finally opened up.

That last thought stopped him. Would she lean into his embrace? Or would his touch snap her out of her confession and drive her away? It wasn't worth the risk to find out. So he fisted his hands at his sides and listened.

"The wealth didn't last. After he died and Aunt Norine came to collect Johanna and me, we found out that he'd maxed out his credit, held two mortgages on the house and hadn't paid on loans for his car in months. He used money to control, to manipulate."

A piece of the puzzle slid into place. Her aversion to money, her insistence on paying for everything. No wonder she had reacted to the teddy bear with such disdain. He'd taken her lack of enjoyment personally, a rejection of him and his attempt to start being a part of their child's life. And she hadn't wanted to be manipulated by lavish gifts.

"He sounds like an ass."

His bald comment startled a small laugh from her.

She glanced over her shoulder, the sunlight playing with her dark hair and creating beautiful streaks of orangish gold that brought out the rosiness in her cheeks. She looked as she had last night when she'd smiled up at Suzie—soft. Warm. Alive.

How had he ever thought her cold?

"My early years with him were pleasant." She started to circle around the room, eyes roving over everything but him. "Picnics on the lakeshore. Train rides around Europe. Summers at beach resorts. He and my mother were happy." She stopped by a globe in the corner, the map covered with little red *C*s that marked the location of a Cabrera business, and ran a finger over the blue of an ocean. "Until they weren't. Until my mother realized she, and I, were nothing more than passing fancies. The more she held on, the more my father tried to escape through spending sprees and other women." She spun the globe, eyes focused on the earth as it revolved. "He loved new things, the more expensive the better. So he tried to appease her with things he thought would make her happy. Jewelry. Clothes. A new car. And all she wanted was his love."

Beneath her detached recitation of her parents' failed marriage, he caught something else.

"What did you want, Calandra?"

Silence descended, save for the soft whish of the globe as it spun.

And then, so softly he almost didn't hear it: "The same thing."

He moved to her then, reached out and took her limp hand in his. When she didn't look, didn't respond to his touch, he gave in to a desire he'd never experienced before and laid his fingers gently on her cheek, guiding her face up until her eyes met his.

Eyes that had turned steely once more. Except this time he wasn't going to back away. Not when he knew so much more about her, about why one minute she was passion incarnate and the next disappeared behind her icy exterior. He'd seen in it in her eyes last night, felt it in her lips beneath his, heard it the tiny sigh that had set his body aflame with desire.

She wanted him. She wanted him just as badly as he wanted her.

"How is wanting lovemaking the same mistake as your mother?"

"She died," Calandra said flatly. "I loved her. But by the end she was weak. She left two daughters alone with a father who treated us more like dolls to be dressed up in couture as a sign of his prominence instead of his children." Her free hand drifted to her stomach, fingers splaying across her belly. "I will never let my child experience the pain of being abandoned."

"And you think I would abandon it?"

Her face twisted into a frown of confusion. "I did... I don't know..." A heavy sigh escaped her lips. "I don't know what to think anymore, Alejandro. You tie me up in knots and I can't think straight."

Focus. Focus on the fact that she wasn't running away, that she wasn't pushing him out, and not on how she had, at least at one point, thought he would abandon their child once he got bored. That someone else thought so little of him.

Although, his mind argued, he had brought it on himself. Until recently, Calandra had seen mainly what he'd allowed the world to see. A carousing billionaire without a care in the world. Few saw the serious side, the dedicated CEO, the hard worker. Easier, and more fun, to live up to the expectation of not doing much except partying his life away.

Safer, too, if he was being completely honest with himself. Safer than trying and risking failure. Hurt. Rejection.

"Let's take a break from the serious talk." For her sake, he assured himself. Not because he was trying to avoid confronting unpleasant truths of his own. "But know this, Calandra—I will never abandon our child."

No scoffing. No roll of the eyes. Just the slightest nod that filled him with relief and a touch of panic. What if he couldn't fulfill that promise? What if he did fail and hurt not just his child, but Calandra, too?

Calandra yawned, and he jumped onto the reprieve she offered. "I'll escort you back to your room so you can get some sleep. We have a busy day tomorrow."

"Where are we going, anyway?" she asked as he tugged her toward the door.

"It's a surprise." One that, despite his inner turmoil, he was very grateful he'd planned out given her revelations tonight. "Trust me."

CHAPTER SIXTEEN

CALANDRA KEPT HER eyes focused on the passing scenery and tried to keep her thoughts, and her gaze, off Alejandro as he guided the car through the French countryside. She'd awoken that morning feeling surprisingly refreshed after her confession and, after seeing she had a text from him asking how she was feeling, giddy. *Giddy.* A giddiness she couldn't shake no matter how sternly she talked to her reflection in the mirror as she'd gotten ready.

He'd been waiting outside the villa, looking like he'd walked straight out of a fashion ad in black jeans and a dark blue polo shirt fitted perfectly to his broad chest and muscular arms. The car ride had been surprisingly relaxing as they talked about everything from their past travels to his favorite movies and her favorite books.

Alejandro gestured to the north. A village perched on a hilltop, the collection of white stone buildings arranged in a charming cluster on the mountainside.

"The village of Gordes."

"It's lovely."

"Glad you like it."

"Did you think I wouldn't?"

"Most women I've known wouldn't enjoy this. They would want something fancy."

"Sounds like most women you know are stuck-up."

"Pretty much." That thousand-watt plastic smile flashed, not the genuine grin or teasing twist of his lips. "They date me because they want the fantasy, not the reality."

Sadness crept over her.

"Is that what you think, Alejandro? That if they knew the real you they wouldn't want you?"

The smile faltered, a slip in his carefree mask that spoke volumes.

He didn't answer. Awkwardness filled the space between them until all she wanted to do was escape the car and disappear down one of the little cobblestone streets she spied. They continued on past Gordes as the sun rose in the sky. Surely they were close to wherever Alejandro was taking them. She needed to get out, stretch her legs and have some time to think.

Why was Alejandro hiding behind this pretense of being spoiled? In the years she'd known him, she would have described him as one of the most confident, self-assured men she knew. Yet she'd seen the cracks in his persona this week, as well as views of a man who intrigued her, who made her long for more than just a hot tryst in a hotel room.

Or on a yacht, her mind taunted.

She thrust that thought away and reflected on what she'd seen of Alejandro this week. The man she'd seen onboard *La Reina* with a deep passion for his work. The man who stood up to his father on her behalf even after she'd hurt him. The man who watched classic movies with his mother and wanted to go into business with his brothers because he respected their work. In the moments he'd tried to impress her with his wealth, the similarities with her father and her genuine disinterest in having anything in common with his previous paramours had helped her stay aloof.

It was the moments when he hadn't tried that had broken through her resolve to keep him at arm's length. When she'd seen the man he was beneath the money and glamour.

The hill on the right sloped down, and the sight before her drew her out of her reverie. She gasped.

"Oh!"

She'd heard of the legendary lavender fields of Provence. But she wasn't prepared for the stunning beauty of it in person. A stone church sat at the base of tree-covered hills, surrounded by thick bushes nearly bursting with violet-colored flowers lined up, one after another.

"Sénanque Abbey," Alejandro said. "Built in 1148."

They drove by the front two lavender fields, the first a large open area with at least a dozen rows of thick, bushy lavender plants. Across a small bridge and behind a line of trees lay another field, smaller but still boasting the same vibrant purple flowers.

"This is incredible," she breathed.

"One of my mother's favorite sites."

"Thank you, Alejandro. For sharing this with me." She tucked a wisp of hair behind her ear. "I never would have gone to a place like this on my own."

He pulled his sunglasses off and gave her one of those genuine smiles that made her heart flip in her chest.

"Calandra Smythe, are you thanking your arch nemesis?"

His joking tone teased a reluctant smile from her. "I wouldn't describe you as a nemesis. Just a thorn in my side."

"A thorn? How flattering. I would have hoped I might compare to something a bit larger."

"No comment."

He chuckled. "You're certainly good for bringing a man down a peg or two."

"So I've been told." She grabbed her purse off the floor, surprisingly eager to see the abbey and the lavender fields up close.

They walked up the drive, the walls of the abbey growing larger as they neared. She found herself entranced by the ancient stone, the elegantly carved windows and the tower that stood proudly against the backdrop of the tree-covered hills. The soothing scent of the lavender surrounded them, floral and sweet.

"It doesn't seem real," Calandra finally said. "Like a fairy tale." She glanced back at the almost empty parking lot. "I guess not many people know of it."

"They do. Peak tourist season for Provence occurs in July." He shot her a smug smile. "Hence why lavender field excursions for *La Reina*'s guests will occur in late June. Two weeks of exclusive access to some of the most beautiful fields in France, minus the elbowing and clamoring for space among the crowds of tourists."

"Smart." Her eyes softened as she gazed at the abbey. "It's the kind of place you're so grateful to discover, but you don't want too many others to know."

When he slipped his arms around her waist and

pulled her back against his muscular chest, she gave in to temptation and leaned against him.

"I'd like to share something with you."

The seriousness in his tone made her freeze. For a moment she said nothing, her breath caught in her chest. If she said no, she'd be doing what she'd been doing from the beginning—staying safe inside her little fortress of solitude while taking away his chances of proving himself.

If she said yes, the door she'd slowly been opening all week as she'd spent time with him, confided in him, would be flung wide-open. The potential for so much joy. So much heartbreak.

She breathed in deeply and leaned deeper into his embrace.

A heartbeat passed. Then his arms tightened around her and he started to speak.

"I had a good childhood. My mother was incredible, always there for Antonio and me."

"Not Adrian?"

"They didn't have the best relationship for a long time. But it's getting better." He huffed out a breath. "I can't say the same for my father and me. It's always been terrible. My first memory of him is showing him a drawing I'd done when I was about four. He'd just gotten back from one of his trips. He didn't even look, just ruffled my hair as he walked into his study and shut the door."

Her heart ached for the little boy who'd just wanted his father's love. Such a simple thing, and yet one that, at least in her experience, was too much to ask.

"I imagine it wasn't the first time he ignored me, or the second or the third, because I remember grabbing a lamp off the table. It broke all over the floor. My father came out, berated me, put me in time-out. I was in trouble, but I had something I hadn't had before—his attention."

A small group wandered past, chattering in English and snapping photos of everything in sight. Alejandro released her and drew her away, his body angled protectively between her and the tourists as he kept one arm wrapped firmly around her waist. As they walked toward a smaller lavender field, he continued.

"I only misbehaved when he was around. It became a game. What could I do when he was home to get his attention, to make him react. The more I did, the angrier he got. I never did it around my mother, and I don't think he ever told her. We kept at it, me acting out and him losing his temper. Adrian didn't attend Eton until he was fifteen, but Padre sent me there when I was thirteen. He told me point-blank the less he saw of me, the better."

They stopped next to a tree with long, crooked branches and thick leaves that provided welcome shade from the growing heat of the afternoon sun. Alejandro's arm dropped from her waist and he stepped forward, hands tucked in his pockets as he stared at the green hills beyond the abbey.

"One day I came back early for a holiday. My father was with a woman in the library." Anger edged into his voice. "I knew the moment I saw them. I knew that my father had betrayed my mother. When he saw me in the doorway, he became enraged. I accused him of cheating on her. He said if I ever told my mother, he would deny everything, insist that I was lying and acting out the way I always had. I had no intention of telling her—she loves him." The smile that crossed his face was almost cruel in its harshness. "So I decided to punish him instead. Breaking lamps was nothing compared to what I would do the rest of his life."

The parallel between his parents and hers, between how he'd threatened his father and her last conversation with hers, made the ache in her chest intensify. She knew exactly what that moment felt like, when one discovered that a parent had committed such a grievous sin against the other.

"I mentioned my father presents a priggish front. He grew up from nothing, so he's obsessed with the image he maintains. Every article that's published, every photo that's snapped, is just another knife in his chest."

It was almost surreal, this glimpse into what could have been her life had Father not died a week after Mom's funeral. Would she have pursued his punishment so zealously? Crafted her entire life around reminding him of his transgressions every chance she got? While she'd never wished him dead, she found herself grateful for the silver lining his death had granted her.

"What does your mother think?"

"Not a fan of the parties." A fond smile temporarily chased away the gloom that had settled over his handsome features. "We were so close, though, that when I started to make the papers, she asked if I was happy. Probably knew I wasn't, but knew me well enough not to push. I wasn't doing anything illegal. I overheard her tell my father once she thought I needed to find myself." His bark of laughter startled a bird out of the tree. It tweeted its dismay, spread its wings and soared up into the summer sky.

"She sounds like a good mom."

"She was. Summers when I was off from school, we watched *The Black Pirate* with Douglas Fairbanks and *The Court Jester* with Danny Kaye. My father discouraged rough play. My mother and Diego, our butler, strung up a rope in the backyard so Antonio and I could pretend we were pirates and swing off one of the trees into the pool."

"That sounds wonderful," Calandra said with a touch of longing.

"It was." He scrubbed a hand over his face. "It should have been enough. But for whatever reason, I wasn't able to let go of this fixation with my father. By the time I graduated from Eton, we barely spoke. When I graduated from Oxford, Padre put me in charge of the weakest of all his holdings—Cabrera Shipping. Five ships, three of them rusty and behind on maintenance. Crews full of dissatisfied men working long hours for horrid pay. He'd given Adrian Cabrera Wines. Antonio was a year behind me at Oxford and had already interned for some luxury resort, so he was in line to head the hospitality management side of Cabrera holdings. Javier had to give me something to save face with the outside world."

"But you turned Cabrera Shipping into a success."

"I pointed out the same thing to Javier about a year ago. He said he'd given me everything to make Cabrera a success and that anyone could have made it profitable." He laughed, the sound hollow. "It shouldn't have made an impression, but it did." He let out a long, slow breath. "I spent the majority of my life acting out, breaking the rules, for my father. First to get his attention. Then to punish him. Every time I ended up in the papers, every time my picture was splashed across some magazine, I got a phone call or a text from him. It embarrassed him. Not being embarrassed mattered more to him than being a part of our family. So I did it more."

Sunlight kissed his cheekbones, highlighting his chiseled features, the strength in his jaw. A man so handsome and yet hurting so deeply it twisted her heart. How many times had she dismissed him as her boss's spoiled little brother? She'd been clinging to her own pain and prejudice so tightly she hadn't been able to look past the surface.

"And here we are." Alejandro spread his hands. "The spoiled, billionaire playboy who wanted to get his father's attention through sex, parties and alcohol. Except the last year I've realized that my hard-earned reputation that was designed to punish my father instead kept me from pursuing what I really wanted. I enjoyed my work for Cabrera. I worked hard to make it a success. But again, to prove my father wrong. So I went after what I wanted."

His eyes fell to her, then drifted down to her stomach.

"Once I set my mind to something, I'm invested." He took a step closer, then another. Her heart jumped into her throat at the raw emotion in his eyes. Sadness, anger and need. "I want to be the father mine never was. That includes being there for our child."

His words settled deep into her bones. In that moment, she knew he meant every word. If she could let herself trust him, be just as vulnerable with him as he'd been with her, their child could grow up with two parents who adored it.

Was it too selfish to hope that, perhaps, there was a possibility for them, too?

CHAPTER SEVENTEEN

A RUMBLING CUT through her thoughts. She stepped out from under the tree branches and looked up as stone-colored clouds raced over the hilltop to the west. A brisk wind barreled down the hillside and whipped the lavender bushes into a frenzy.

Alejandro grabbed her hand.

"Time to go."

They hurried to the car, the first cool drops of rain hitting her skin as he opened the door for her. He ran around the front of the car and got in just as the clouds released a torrent of rain so thick they could barely see ten feet in front of them. She pulled out her phone and checked the weather forecast.

"Rain for hours. And possible hail."

"There's a bed-and-breakfast nearby we can take shelter at."

Alejandro's words cut through the thundering of the rain as he pulled out of the parking lot. Her hands tightened on the seat of the car, grasping at anything that would anchor her even as her breathing quickened.

"A bed-and-breakfast?" she repeated in as casual a voice as she could muster. "Sure."

They stayed silent as Alejandro drove at a crawl

through the summer squall. It gave her time to think. Too much time. Alejandro had just opened up and shared himself with her. Not the hints and bites of information he'd been giving her throughout the week, but a baring of his soul.

She no longer wondered if she was in love with him. She knew. Now she just needed to know what to do next.

Five minutes and one winding road up a hillside later and they pulled under the awning of L'Auberge de la Lavande.

They walked through the double glass doors into the lobby. Calandra kept her mouth from dropping open. When she heard the words *bed-and-breakfast* or *inn*, as the sign on the outside had proclaimed, she thought of quilt-covered beds, pancakes and a long porch with rocking chairs.

The Lavender Inn catered to an entirely different clientele. The lobby boasted dark wooden floors polished to a shine beneath the lamps dripping with crystals that had been artfully scattered among white and lavender-colored furniture. Elegant armchairs, chaise lounges and a few sofas offered rest and places to visit. The walls were covered in professional photographs of the lavender fields, the abbey and the village of Gordes. One side of the lobby was glass that she guessed, on a sunny day, provided incredible views of the valley beneath the inn.

Even the air carried the faint, floral scent.

A sweet-faced girl in a violet suit jacket and starched white shirt smiled at them.

"Bonjour."

"Bonjour," Alejandro replied. "Do you have any rooms available?"

The girl smiled, her cheeks dimpling. "You're in luck! We were all booked, but we just had a cancellation for our honeymoon suite."

"Honeymoon suite?" Calandra repeated.

The girl nodded enthusiastically. "Top floor. Once the rain passes, you'll have the best view of the lavender field from a private balcony."

"I don't think—"

"Perfect," Alejandro interrupted as he passed the clerk a credit card. "Monsieur and Madame Cabrera, please."

His casual use of such a title made her want to laugh and cry at the same time. Laugh, because a week ago she would have shuddered at the thought of Alejandro being involved in her child's life, much less being tied to him herself.

Cry, because in the last couple of days, she'd thought more and more of what it would be like to have Alejandro not just in their child's life but in *her* life.

After checking in, Alejandro guided her to the elevator. The doors swooshed open, and she paused. The last time they'd gotten into an elevator, they hadn't been able to keep their hands off each other.

"I promise not to kiss you this time."

"But what if I want you to?"

The words slipped out before she could stop them. She sneaked a glance at Alejandro. He stood next to her, his body tight, eyes straight forward. Her throat constricted. Had she waited too long?

"Are you sure?"

Those three words, the barely constrained passion

in his dark, sensual voice, broke down the last remaining threads of her defenses. Confidence emboldened her to walk into the elevator, turn and meet his eyes, allowing him to see the naked desire in her own gaze.

"You coming?"

Her breath hitched as he stalked toward her, eyes on fire as his presence filled the elevator. The door slid shut.

He started to reach for her. But she didn't want to leave any doubt in his mind that she was initiating, that she wanted him. She moved forward, pushed him against the wall of the elevator, slid her arms around his neck and kissed him.

Just like that, she was tumbling, falling deeper into the complicated mess of emotions she felt toward this man. Yet instead of being afraid, she threw caution to the wind as her fingers tangled in his hair and she wantonly pressed her body against his.

What have I done?

One last rational thought pounded through her head before Alejandro groaned and leaned in. His tongue swept the seam of her lips. She opened her mouth, moaned when he tasted her.

Without stopping their frantic kissing, Alejandro grabbed her hips, turned and pressed her against the wall. The firmness of his erection pressed against her thighs. She wriggled against him, sliding her core up and down his length with wanton abandon.

"Stop!"

The whispered word penetrated the haze of desire. She reared back, humiliation creeping in. She was very inexperienced, but she'd thought, based on their last time, that she'd at least pleased him.

Alejandro grabbed her face between his hands and rested his forehead against hers, his breathing labored.

"If you keep doing that, I'm not going to last."

The thrill of knowing she had that kind of effect on him emboldened her. She twisted, wrapped her legs around his waist and brought her body flush against his. She brazenly rubbed herself against his length, moaning as he hardened even more beneath her.

"Then I guess you better find a way to distract me."

Before he could respond, the elevator dinged and the doors whooshed open. She got a brief impression of a four-poster bed with gauzy curtains and a vine-covered balcony before he whisked her inside.

Where this fire, this passion came from, she couldn't say. But she loved it, this side of her that she'd only let out once to play. Loved seeing his eyes darken, feeling his shoulders tighten beneath her fingers.

He took up her challenge. And devoured her.

Before she could do anything else, he hooked his fingers in the straps of her dress and pulled them down, baring her breasts to his hungry gaze. Then he wrapped his strong arms around her body and pulled her against him. She cried out, the sensation of her bare nipples rubbing against his chest making her throb with need.

"Alejandro, please…"

He kissed her once more, keeping her arms pinned to her sides. His lips trailed over her jaw, up to her ear, where he placed the most delicate of kisses before sucking the lobe into his hot mouth and nibbling. She nearly came apart then and there.

But he was just getting started. As she moaned and begged and writhed, he pulled her onto his lap and continued his sensual onslaught, dragging his mouth down her neck with excruciating slowness, over the pulse beating wildly in her throat. Fire burned at every spot his lips touched, sparks skipping over her skin, making her feel feverish with need.

And then he sucked a nipple into his mouth. She arched against him, cried out his name. He released one of her arms to cup her other breast in his hand, his fingers cupping her flesh and stroking it with long, skillful caresses. He continued to suck and nip and nibble and kiss until she was almost sobbing.

Then he moved to the other, repeating the same sensuous seduction as she rubbed herself against him, that fire building and building until she couldn't stand it anymore and came apart. She fell against him, shuddering, her free hand tangled in his hair.

He softened his caresses, gently kissing the globes of her breasts as she drifted back down from the incredible heights he'd sent her to.

"Alejandro... I..."

He kissed her on the lips, silencing whatever she'd been about to say. Then he moved her off his lap onto the bed and stood. She huffed in protest.

Until he grabbed the dress gathered about her waist, tugged it down along with her underwear and tossed it to the side.

Leaving her completely naked.

She started to cover herself, to cross her legs and cover her breasts with her arms. He caught one of her hands in his, brought it to his lips and kissed her fingers.

"Do you trust me?"

Trust. It always came back to trust between the two of them. Could he trust her to give him a fair chance at being a parent? Could she trust him to not repeat the sins of her father and hurt her, hurt their child?

Yes. Yes, she could. This man trusted her. Not just with her job, but with his secrets, his past, his hopes and dreams. He wanted to be a good father, a partner, and she loved him for it.

Slowly, she nodded.

He knelt between her legs. He stroked the folds of her most intimate skin with one finger, sliding up and down with a light touch that drove her crazy.

"Alejandro…please…"

Her hips bucked as his finger touched her *there*. Then he pulled back, and she whimpered. A whimper followed by a cry as he leaned down and replaced his finger with his mouth. His tongue moved over, dancing over her skin as heat pulsed through her, carrying her higher as she tangled her fingers in his hair and begged for release.

He slid a finger inside her, her heat clenching down around him. He sucked her into his mouth, and she came apart again. Her entire body shattered, sensation rippling over her skin as she closed her eyes against the pinwheels of light dancing in her vision.

Her body went limp, the coolness of the sheets a pleasing contrast against her heated body. Her heart pounded against her ribs. Slowly, with deep, cleansing breaths, her lust receded.

"Calandra…"

She opened her eyes to see him braced above her, that devilish smirk lurking on his lips.

"See what happens when you trust me?"

If he hadn't just given her such pleasure, she'd be tempted to do something utterly childish, like pinch him. Instead, she sat up, reached forward and laid her hand on the growing bulge in his pants, savoring the darkening of his eyes as he let out a hiss. "What are you doing?"

"Do you trust me?"

He groaned as she tightened her grasp on him.

"Guess I'll have to."

She unzipped his pants, her fingers curling around his thick length. He sucked in a breath. His eyes blazed as he watched her hand slide up and down, trailing over every inch of him.

And then she leaned down to suck him into her mouth. He groaned, his fingers tangling in her hair. She loved the taste of him, the musky, masculine scent. It made her feel wild, passionate, *free*.

"Calandra…"

He stood and removed his clothes. Then he sat next to her on the bed, picked her up and tugged her onto his lap. He paused, the tip of his sex resting against her core.

"Calandra…" She started to ease down, but he stopped her. "You need to know—"

"No conversation," she whispered as she tried to sink down. She needed him inside her, needed to feel him.

"London."

The word stopped her cold. She stared down at him, hurt and jealousy splashing cold water on her lust.

"What about London?"

His fingers tightened on her thighs. "Nothing happened. It's only been you. Ever since New York. No one but you."

Her heart burst. She slid down his length, then

leaned forward, pressed her naked skin against his and kissed him with all the love and desire she could pour into a single act. He kissed her back, fingers tangling in her hair as he marked her as his.

Then she sat up and moved, slowly at first, relearning his body, how he felt inside her. His hands stayed on her hips, his eyes fixed on hers as she rode him.

She burst once more, a kaleidoscope of colors obscuring her vision as she arched back and cried out his name. He jerked against her, returned her call with one of his own as he groaned her name, then shuddered. She collapsed against him, keeping at bay all the wild, rational thoughts trying to maneuver their way in.

For now, just for a little while, she wanted to savor this moment when she'd thrown off the shackles of her past and embraced the present.

And the man who, no matter how hard she had tried, was now firmly lodged deep inside her heart.

CHAPTER EIGHTEEN

A LIGHT AWAKENED ALEJANDRO. He opened his eyes to see the trumpet flowers on the balcony glowing as the setting sun lit them from behind. A quick glance confirmed the bed was empty. Concerned, he threw back the covers, tugged on his discarded pants and padded over to the glass doors, his heartbeat slowing as he spied Calandra on the cream-colored divan on the balcony.

Long legs, bare and sleek. That incredible body wrapped in a lavender bathrobe, the top parted just enough to hint at her stunning breasts. Her face, smooth and serene, eyelashes dark against her skin, eyes closed.

Sexy, yes. Sensual. Beautiful. But it wasn't just her beauty that drew him in. It was her strength, the gentle nature she hid from all but the privileged few who got to see her commitment and loyalty.

When they'd gazed at the abbey, standing almost in the exact spot he remembered first viewing those ancient walls with his mother, a sense of rightness had settled over him. Just as Calandra had envisioned taking their child to the top of the Eiffel Tower, he saw himself standing with his son or daughter in the midst of the lavender, their tiny hand engulfed in his grasp.

That vision had included Calandra by his side. Where she was meant to be.

So he'd done what he'd been pushing her to do all week—he'd opened up. Told her everything. Either she could accept him, all of him, or she couldn't.

Yes, she'd initiated sex. She'd responded with even more wild abandon, more passion than he had ever dreamed of.

But for the first time, sex wasn't enough. He needed her to trust him, to believe him capable of managing whatever life they were going to forge together as much as she believed in his ability to make *La Reina* a success.

He distracted himself from his tumultuous thoughts by tugging his phone out of his pocket and checking his email. An update that one of the new ships was on track to be completed next month, pending a final inspection. Another about how the news of the impending new ship had spread and seventy-two percent of their cargo space had been booked in the past twenty-four hours alone, with more calls coming in.

All excellent news. More positives he could bring to the meeting and the vote on Saturday. Already he'd received emails congratulating him from three of the seven board members. Just one more on his side and he'd be clear.

So why could he not focus? Why, when everything he wanted was within reach, was he so distracted?

Distracted by the woman out on the balcony who had worked her way into his heart long ago and he was only just now realizing it? He'd been falling for her for years. It had taken a night of incredible, mind-blowing, soul-searing sex and an unexpected child to make him realize that how he felt about her went far deeper than casual attraction.

Yet still she held back.

Calandra opened her eyes, not seeing him in the shadows beyond the door. She stood and slowly moved to the edge of the balcony, her back to him. Drawn like a moth to a flame, he stood and walked out onto the balcony, his eyes fixed on her. Her shoulders tensed with every step he took.

She didn't look back at him, just kept her eyes trained on the lavender fields laid out below them. The setting sun bathed the fields in a golden light that made the flowers glow like violet fire.

One of the most romantic places he'd ever been. His hand started to come up, to slide around Calandra's waist and pull her against him, savor the warmth of her body. A natural reaction to being in such a relaxed setting with an attractive woman by his side.

The urge to press a kiss to her hair, to slide his hand around and let it rest over the gentle swell of her stomach, was unnatural.

Without Alejandro Cabrera, international playboy extraordinaire, he didn't know who to be. But every time he thought about Calandra, not as an employee or business partner, but as a woman, as the mother of his child, he saw whom he wanted to become.

Calandra closed her eyes and leaned back into Alejandro's embrace. She forced herself to breathe as she felt the warmth of his body kiss her skin.

"I remember as a child I was afraid of heights."

She let her hands settle over his and opened her eyes, savoring the incredible landscape before her. "I'm so glad I overcame that."

"I won't let you fall."

Too late. I've already fallen.

His words made her want to melt. For years, she'd been the one to keep Johanna safe. Aunt Norine had been a wonderful guardian, but her age, coupled with her health, had made Calandra the one who ensured Johanna got off to school in the morning, who helped with cleaning and other chores around the house. She'd been in charge ever since she was seven and Mother had stopped getting out of bed. It had gotten lonely, leading all the time. But she'd gotten used to it.

Until now. Until now when this man cradled her in his arms like she was the most delicate of treasures. When the slightest touch seared her skin.

When he'd opened his heart to her.

"I told you that my father was larger than life. He also had a proclivity for living to the fullest. At least that's how he'd termed it."

Words she'd never thought she'd express bubbled up inside her, threatened to suffocate her as they piled up in her throat. She'd kept everything inside for so long. People had labeled her stuck-up and bitchy when she kept her distance. Gradually, she came to think of herself as such. Cold, calculating, unsympathetic. Once in a while she experienced a flash of emotion. But she kept to herself because she didn't know how to handle them, how to be anything but detached. Detached was safe. Detached was bulletproof.

Detached was lonely. And the more time she spent around Alejandro, the more she suspected she had done herself a great disservice living so distantly from other human beings.

As if he sensed the dark place she'd slipped into, he pressed a kiss to her cheek.

Strength. He gave her strength.

"I don't know when my mother found out he was cheating. I do know that around the time I turned seven, she started to fade. Didn't come down as often to meals, didn't go out on family drives. My father also started spending more and more time away. I would get up in the morning, bring tea to my mother and beg her to drink something. She eventually would, but I usually had to cry to get her to." She blinked hard. "I remember the first magazine one of the girls brought in. A photo of Dad getting out of a car in Bora Bora, a young lady in the front seat with him, his secretary. He had his hand up, like he was trying to cover up the camera lens."

She could still see the woman in her mind's eyes, the tiny red dress, the sky-high heels.

"I was upset. I wanted to be comforted, to have my mother tell me that our family was still okay. So I took the magazine to her. She said she'd asked my father about it, too, that he'd insisted it was a business trip. But over time there were more photos. I stopped bringing the magazines to her, because every time I did, she got weaker."

She gripped his hands, soaked up the warmth of his skin, as her voice grew thick. "When I was nine, Johanna was born. I don't know what happened between Mom and Dad, but just before and for about six months after, they were happy again." Amazing how clearly she could remember sitting on Dad's lap, smell his spicy aftershave as he helped her hold baby Johanna wrapped in a soft pink blanket. Mom had looked on from her bed, a rosy glow in her cheeks and a sparkle in her eyes.

"It didn't last. Nothing did with Dad. Around the time Johanna turned one, he started going out again. Filled his absences with toys for Johanna and me, gifts for Mom. Every time one of those gift boxes arrived, she faded a little more. One night I heard Johanna screaming." Her throat constricted so tightly she nearly choked. "I found her in her bassinet, wet and cold. No blanket. Mom had started taking sleeping pills. She slept right through it."

Alejandro's arms tightened around her waist.

"So I started taking care of Johanna. And Mom."

"What about servants?"

It was almost a shock, hearing Alejandro's voice after she'd been speaking so long.

"We had maids and a housekeeper. A cook during the week. But I was ashamed. Ashamed of my father for abandoning us. Ashamed of my mother for abandoning us, too, in her own way. So I did what I could by myself."

She closed her eyes. Exhaustion and memories tugged at her, made her weary.

"I remember the last night I had with her. I was twelve. Johanna was three. I took her to Mom's room for a visit and Mom was…happy." Her eyes grew hot and she scrunched her eyes tight against the tears. "I was so…hopeful. She was dressed in this beautiful gown she hadn't worn in years. She'd had the cook bring up treats. There were chocolates and strawberries and ice cream, and she even let me have a sip of champagne." A tear escaped and traced a burning trail down her cheek. "She…she told me she was so proud of me. Her big girl."

Somewhere in the distance, a bird tweeted. She opened her eyes. The sight of the French countryside lit by the warm glow of the sun calmed her racing pulse, tethered her to this moment enough for her to force out her next words.

"We put Johanna to bed together. She tucked me in and kissed my forehead. I thought we would finally go back to the way things were. That I would get to be a kid again. I went to bed happy."

Her voice cracked. Alejandro started to say something, but she plowed forward. "I found her the next morning. She'd overdosed on sleeping pills."

"Calandra…"

He turned her in the circle of his arms and cupped her face. She met his eyes, sucking in one shuddering breath after another.

"She said in her note…that she couldn't go on… any longer." All the emotions she'd suppressed, all the grief she'd stuffed down deep inside, rose up at once, a tidal wave of sorrow that threatened to drown her. "I confronted Dad…after the funeral. He cared more about his reputation and whether anyone knew that she'd killed herself than the fact that his wife had committed suicide because of him. And then a week later… he died. In a car accident with his mistress."

She broke. Years of restrained sobs escaped. Had Alejandro not been holding her, cradling her, she would have sunk to the floor of the balcony.

He scooped her up in his arms, carried her inside and laid her on the bed. She started to reach for him, to ask him to stay, but before she could, he laid down next to her and drew her back into his embrace. How long she cried, she couldn't say. Alejandro stayed by her side the entire time, stroking her hair, kissing her forehead, whispering words in Spanish she didn't understand but still took comfort in.

At last, her tears dried. When she looked into Alejandro's eyes, saw the emotion brimming his dark blue gaze, she couldn't stop herself from kissing him. He paused, as if waiting to see if this was just a reaction to unburdening herself or if she truly wanted him.

She smiled against his mouth. Then sat up, rolled and straddled his hips.

His eyes flared. "Calandra…"

She leaned down and pressed her lips to his again. She nipped his bottom lip, thrilled at the groan that escaped him as his hands gripped her thighs. With one tug, she loosened the belt of the robe and shrugged out of the sleeves. Seeing his gaze darken with passion as he gazed at her naked body made her feel beautiful, sexy…

Strong.

She reached down, grabbed his hands in hers and guided them to her breasts. His fingers settled on her flesh, sliding down to stroke her nipples into hard points. She gasped, arched, moaned.

"Alejandro…make love to me."

Before she could take a breath, he sat up, one arm circling around her waist, and laid her back onto the bed with a strength that stole her breath. He stripped himself of his clothes in record time and laid his naked body on top of hers. He kissed her as he slid inside her, claiming her body with his.

They moved together, their pace almost frantic as they arched against each other, hands grasping, lips tasting, fire building until they came apart in each other's arms.

As they drifted down from the peak of pleasure, three words rose to her lips. She almost whispered them.

Wait.

Just a little longer. A little more time to think, to process.

Her eyes fluttered shut as he pulled the sheet up over them and she snuggled into his embrace.

"Calandra…"

"Hmm?"

Silence. Then another soft kiss on her temple. "Nothing. Go to sleep."

Something in his tone filtered through, a hesitancy that sent off a distant warning bell. But the satisfaction from their lovemaking, coupled with the events of the day, silenced it, and she drifted off to sleep.

CHAPTER NINETEEN

THE ELEGANT STRAINS of a violin carried across the ballroom of *La Reina*. Sequins sparkled under the light of the chandelier, silk flashed as dancers spun across the floor and champagne bubbled in over a hundred glasses.

"I'm still irritated that you chose champagne over my wine," Adrian said as he took a sip.

Everleigh patted her belly. "And I'm still irritated that I can't drink any of it."

They stood off to the side of the ballroom with Alejandro, watching as guests arrived. Even though the event was designed primarily to show off *La Reina* to the board, Alejandro had followed Adrian's lead from the merger party he and Everleigh had hosted a couple months ago and invited his employees.

"Not too bad." Antonio appeared next to Alejandro and clapped him on the shoulder. "Perhaps we should go into business together more often."

Alejandro smiled as his eyes roamed over the crowds. "Perhaps."

"Looking for someone?"

Adrian's voice was light, but Alejandro didn't miss the edge in his older brother's tone.

"Perhaps."

Everleigh leaned in. "Did you decide what you're going to do?"

Alejandro's eyes snapped to Adrian's face. "You told her?"

"Told her what?" Antonio asked, his gaze swinging back and forth like he was watching a tennis match.

Everleigh blushed. "I'm sorry. He was so irritable in Paris that I pried it out of him."

"I wasn't irritable!" Adrian retorted.

Before his family could drive him nuts, Alejandro walked away. He would deal with his brothers and soon-to-be sister-in-law later. Now, he wanted to find Calandra.

She had truly outdone herself. The food, brochures full of pictures of *La Reina*'s completed rooms and a story about where the ship would be in a year, sprigs of lavender she'd added to the rose centerpieces in a nod to some of the excursions they'd be offering—all of it was better than he could have ever envisioned.

"Alejandro!"

He turned, unable to contain his grin as his mother approached him, arms open wide.

"I'm so proud of you!" she gushed as she hugged him. "You've turned this ship into a marvel."

"*Gracias*, Madre."

He started to say more when a flash of yellow caught his eye. He turned. His heart stopped in his chest.

He hadn't been sure she'd wear it. But after he dropped her off in Marseille to do a final walkthrough of *La Reina* yesterday morning with a heated kiss and a whispered goodbye, his feet had guided him down the lane to the boutique. He'd wanted to give it to her in person, see her face when she opened it. By the time he was done with his own preparations for the party, and he'd cracked open the door to the guest suite, Calandra had been fast asleep. He'd had to settle for leaving the petal-pink box with a white ribbon on the table.

The longing to crawl into bed with her, to wake her with kisses and hear her say his name as he slid inside her again, had been almost unbearable. But something held him back. They hadn't talked the rest of the night in Provence, aside from whispering each other's names as they'd woken sometime around midnight and made love again. Then once more in the morning when they climbed into the shower together and she'd sunk to her knees and taken him in her mouth. He'd nearly come undone before he'd grabbed her by her elbows, lifted her up, wrapped her legs around his waist and thrust inside her as hot water had poured over their naked skin.

The car ride had been spent in pleasant, companionable silence, their fingers woven together. Talk had been unnecessary.

Until they did talk, clarified what this new development meant and how she felt about him, he wouldn't push his luck and risk pushing her away.

Although he'd worried if he'd crossed a boundary by buying her the dress. Now he had his answer.

She'd mentioned the little girl who hid in the shadow of her father, who had continued to hide all her life. But not tonight. Tonight she shone, the yellow of the dress making her skin glow. She'd left her hair unbound, loose curls falling over her shoulders as she made her rounds, whispering a word to a server here and propping up a rose in an arrangement there.

Still the same confidence. Still the same power. Unlike four months ago, though, tonight her shoulders were relaxed. Her movements less rigid, more assured and less tense.

And she smiled. His heart clenched as their eyes met. She glanced down at her dress, then back at him and mouthed *Thank you*.

"You care for her."

His mother startled him out of his musings. He swung his head around, summoning a jovial grin.

"She's a good friend."

"Ah. I didn't realize you were capable of being so discreet."

He arched an eyebrow in her direction. "When have I ever not been discreet?"

She snorted. "The Venetian Hotel…"

"Everyone brings that up."

"The Louvre," she continued.

"A minor misunderstanding."

She shook her head. "I worried about you, you know."

He paused. Her comments had always been sparse on his activities. He loathed the idea that he'd caused her stress. "I'm sorry."

She waved her hand. "I worried. All mothers do. I wondered if you were truly happy. And," she added with a twist of her lips, "I didn't like the insinuations of the tabloids. There's so much more to you than what the world sees."

The same words Calandra had spoken to him. Words that warmed his chest.

Had it been just four months ago? Four months since he'd seen Calandra standing in the midst of the chaos left by Adrian's guests, resolution firming her face even as her shoulders had sagged the tiniest fraction? That night, all he'd wanted to do was help. Be someone's savior, for once, instead of their curse. And the more time he'd spent with her, the more he'd seen something all too familiar.

Someone hiding behind a mask no one bothered to look past.

Perhaps that's why they had such explosive chemistry. In those moments, they didn't just lust after each other and sate their desire with sex. They ripped their masks off for the only other person in the world they could be themselves with.

His eyes drifted to Calandra. He'd felt possessive over *La Reina*, but it was a mere flicker compared to the inferno that blazed anytime he pictured Calandra round with his child.

Doubt slithered into his mind. Was it possible, to go from wanting nothing to do with matrimony a week ago to contemplating a marriage proposal? What if his feelings for Calandra, his desire to be a dad, were misplaced? If *La Reina* succeeded, would he be this focused on being a father?

"Alejandro?"

His father's voice cut through his dark musings and made his spine straighten. Slowly, he turned.

"Padre."

If his mother sensed the sudden tension between father and son, she didn't let on. She crossed to her husband, who took her hands in his and smiled at her like she was the most precious thing in the world.

The look on his mother's face, one of happiness and love, was the only thing that had made him hold his tongue over the years. Made him hold it now despite the red haze of anger that colored his view of the room.

"Good evening, my dear."

"Good evening." Madre kissed him on the cheek, then gestured to the ballroom. "Our son has achieved something wonderful here tonight."

"He has."

Alejandro resisted rolling his eyes. Always an act, always the supportive father in public and his number one critic in private.

"Alejandro, may I have a word?"

He wanted to say no, to tell his father that until the board held their vote at nine o'clock, he had no interest in being within a dozen feet of him.

But with his mother looking on with such pride and exuding pure happiness, he had no choice but to incline his head and follow his father out of the ballroom.

As they walked out, he looked up. Calandra watched him, eyes flitting between them, a frown on her face. He gave her a small smile. Knowing she would be waiting for him gave him a boost, one he desperately needed if he was going to face Javier.

He strode past his father and led the way into an alcove off the grand foyer. He stood off to the side, waited for Javier to follow him inside and then moved in front of the doorway. One wrong word and he was gone. He would not have his night of triumph ruined.

"The board has already informed me of their decision."

His stomach sank, followed by a swift rush of anger. Based on the emails, the conversations he'd had as he circulated the ballroom, he thought they'd vote in favor. The impulsive part of him wanted to turn around, walk back to the ballroom and demand an explanation for their duplicity. Few of them had seen him at his angriest. Perhaps it was time.

"Seems like you won this round, then."

Javier blinked. "What do you mean?"

"Getting the board to vote against *La Reina*." He leaned in, flashing a devil's smile. "No matter. *La Reina* will succeed. All that money you accuse me of wasting has been accumulating a nice bit of interest in a Swiss bank account. More than enough to see her through her first year of operations."

His father frowned. "There's been a misunderstanding. The board is voting unanimously to complete the renovation of *La Reina* and support its opening later this year."

Triumph zinged through his veins. He raised his chin. "I'm glad they saw sense."

Javier clasped his hands behind his back and started to pace. "Is that what you truly think? That I was trying to beat my own son, to make him fail?"

Alejandro bit back the first words he wanted to utter. He tucked his hands in his pockets and leaned against one of the pillars.

"When have you ever given me cause to believe otherwise?"

Javier sagged. Suddenly, his father looked very old, his wrinkles deepening as he sank down onto a settee and hung his head. Alejandro never would have guessed himself capable of pity for his sire. But the sight of the patriarch of the Cabrera empire, shoulders drooped, skin gray, inspired just that.

"I've been too hard on you."

He must have misheard.

"What?"

Javier scrubbed a hand over his face. "I was a terrible father to you. To your brothers." He let out a hoarse laugh. "I don't even know why your mother stayed with me."

"I don't, either. How long did you cheat on her?" Javier's head snapped up. "Or are you cheating on her still?"

"No!"

His father's denial echoed down the foyer. Alejandro arched a brow.

"Careful, Padre. Unless you want to draw attention to who you really are."

"Who I…"

Javier's voice trailed off as his eyes widened slightly. "Minerva."

"Minerva?"

"The woman you saw me with in the library." Javier swallowed. "You're right. I cheated on your mother."

Cold anger chilled his veins and tightened his fists. He'd known for years. But hearing the confirmation elevated his hatred to a new level.

"Although not the time you saw me."

Alejandro barked a laugh. "Does it matter?"

"It does." Javier hung his head. "You know your mother lost a child, a daughter, between you and Adrian, yes?" At Alejandro's nod, he continued. "I loved…love," he corrected, "your brother. You. Antonio."

The closest his father had ever come to saying "I love you."

"But I'd really looked forward to having a girl." Another emotion he'd never expected to see on his father's face: sorrow. "When we lost the baby…your mother retreated into herself. And I buried myself in work." He stared down at the floor, lost in memory. "Losing a baby wasn't as talked about back then. It's not an excuse for how I behaved. It just…counseling, mental health, they weren't as accepted.

"When your mother got pregnant with you, she barely got out of bed. The doctor encouraged her to rest. But she was so scared that she hardly ever left her room. And then I met Minerva. It's because of her that I worried about the women you associated with." He scrubbed a hand over his face. "I met Minerva at a hotel bar. I'd been drinking. A lot. Before I knew it, we went back to my room and…" He waved a hand in the air. "One time. The biggest mistake of my life."

"I don't believe you."

"Because you saw us together at our house in Granada? Yes, I can see why." He ran a hand through his hair. Hair that, Alejandro now noticed, was thinning at the top.

"Minerva, it turns out, wanted more. Much more. I told her in the morning that I had made a mistake. I told her about losing the baby, your mother being pregnant with you, everything. She didn't care. She wanted a ring on her finger. And if she couldn't get that, she wanted money."

Alejandro arched a brow. "She blackmailed you?"

Javier nodded once. "For almost twenty years, until I found evidence that she had embezzled funds from a charity she managed. A stalemate, but I haven't heard from her in thirteen years. The day you found us in the library, she had just upped her demands and provided a picture she'd taken of us in bed together while I'd been asleep."

Alejandro's stomach rolled. Such a photo would ruin his mother.

"Every time I saw you…knowing that my weakness had led to such a mistake, I could barely look at you. When you started to act out more, I saw myself in you." His lips quirked up into a sad smile. "I became determined to make sure you didn't duplicate my mistakes. So instead of focusing on the good, I came down hard. The more you misbehaved, the harder I tried to correct you."

"You didn't just come down hard." He hadn't even known himself capable of the wrath that infused his voice. "You abandoned me, then brought me to my lowest point."

"I'm sorry, son."

"Sorry?"

Javier stood, slowly, as if a great weight rested on his shoulders.

"What else can I say? I'm sorry I placed the burden of my mistakes on your shoulders so young. That I pushed you into the life you lead now." Javier huffed. "Ironically enough, turned you into me."

A hum started in his head, low but steadily building to a roar.

"What do you mean?"

"I was just like you when I met your mother. Different women, clubs, spending money left and right."

Just like your father.

The world tilted. His father might be making amends now, but that didn't erase decades of pain. Madre had often spoken of how quickly they'd fallen in love, how absolutely certain they both had been about their future together.

Just like him and Calandra.

"I hope if you ever have children, son, you can avoid the many, many mistakes I've made." Javier took a tentative step forward. "Chief among them ever making you doubt that I didn't want you to succeed. I was harsh. Unnecessarily so. I wanted you to succeed, wanted you to be the man I knew you could be."

If the situation wasn't so sad, he would laugh. Finally, he had an explanation, an apology, even words of support from his father.

Words that had come at a price. He'd based his entire existence, the man he was today, on what had transpired in that library. And for what? Nothing. And now he had to confront the possibility that, if he continued to pursue a life with Calandra, he would fall into the same trap his father had. Trying to turn himself into someone capable of love, fidelity, fatherhood, only to fail and leave Calandra broken, just as her father had done to her mother, and their child alone, just as he'd been. Just as Calandra had been because of the sins of her father.

"What if I can't break the cycle?"

He hadn't meant to utter the words aloud. They echoed in the stillness.

Javier gazed at him with sad eyes. "You're a strong man. You're capable."

"But if I can't?" Alejandro demanded, his voice hoarse.

His father breathed in deeply. "If you can't, then don't get married. Don't have children. Don't risk hurting a woman who deserves none of the pain men like us are capable of causing. If you don't know for sure that you want that in your life, then it's not worth it."

CHAPTER TWENTY

THE YELLOW MUSLIN whispered over Calandra's skin as she moved about the ballroom, the fabric as soft as a lover's touch, as delicate as butterfly wings. When she'd seen herself in the mirror for the first time, she couldn't stop the smile from breaking across her face.

When she worked for Cabrera Wines, she'd been based in New York, and she'd shopped at the same designer's store on Madison Avenue. A wonderfully competent saleswoman named Brittany had known her preferences: dark colors, clean lines and simple silhouettes. The clothing had made her feel powerful, in control and, when needed, it gave her the ability to fade in the background and let her work take center stage.

Now, for the second time in her life, she felt beautiful. Not authoritative, not proficient, but feminine, lovely.

If she'd known herself capable of this level of happiness, she would have let down her walls much sooner. *La Reina*'s event was a success. Judging by the whispers she overhead as she'd walked around the ballroom, the board would vote in Alejandro's favor.

And tonight, after the meeting, she would tell Alejandro she loved him. The attraction that had taken root in New York had only strengthened. Except last night it been more than just physical attraction. That blind trust had reached out and ensnared her, heart and soul.

Because she wasn't just counting down the days until she could fly home, check in hand and Alejandro out of her life. No, she was dreaming of her and Alejandro, standing together, a baby cradled between them as he kissed her on the forehead.

Because I'm in love.

As soon as she'd seen the box, she'd known what was inside. She'd reverently undone the bow and unwrapped the tissue paper. Her first glimpse of the sunshine-yellow fabric had brought tears to her eyes.

When she donned the gown, along with the accompanying silver sandals, she'd never felt so beautiful in her entire life. She'd even twirled in front of the mirror. Johanna wouldn't have believed it even if she'd seen it.

She glanced around the ballroom. Adrian and Everleigh were off to the side. Judging by Everleigh's failed attempts at covertly glancing at her stomach, Adrian had told her about the baby.

The older woman she'd seen in Paris was with them, too. She caught Calandra's eye and raised her champagne glass with a smile. Calandra cautiously smiled back. Had Alejandro told her about them? About the baby?

Although there wasn't really a "them" to speak of yet. Yes, they'd had another incredible night of sex. They'd shared their deepest secrets. They'd held hands on the drive back to Marseille and he'd gifted her this beautiful dress.

Uncertainty flickered through her. He wanted to

be involved with the baby. She thought she'd seen the same emotion, the same passion in his eyes.

But he hadn't said it. His voice, too, just before they'd fallen asleep at the inn, lurked on the edges of her memory. He'd been on the verge of saying something.

Stop.

She was borrowing trouble. The meeting would happen in an hour. Then she'd tell him how she felt.

Five minutes later, Alejandro still hadn't reappeared with his father. A quick glance confirmed everything was continuing smoothly. After a quick word to the assistant she'd hired for the evening from a local agency—one she'd strongly recommend Alejandro hire full-time—she walked out of the ballroom.

He doesn't need rescuing.

No, Alejandro most certainly could handle himself. But he didn't have to face his father and whatever eleventh-hour obstacle he was trying to throw in his path.

The low murmur of voices reached her ears. As she continued down the grand foyer, they grew louder. She started to call out when Alejandro's voice, harsh with anguish, echoed down the hall.

"What if I can't break the cycle?"

Cycle? Had something else happened to the ships in construction?

"You're a strong man. You're capable."

Unexpected words from Javier.

"But if I can't?"

She continued forward, ready to break in, to tell Javier once and for all to end his attacks on his middle son.

And then the older Cabrera's words froze her in place.

"If you can't, then don't get married. Don't have children. Don't risk hurting a woman who deserves none of the pain men like us are capable of causing. If you don't know for sure that you want that in your life, then it's not worth it."

She waited for Alejandro's rebuttal, for him to tell Javier that he was indeed having a child, that he and Calandra had discovered something special in the midst of their mutually painful histories.

Each beat of silence drove the stake deeper into her heart. Her vision blurred, and for a moment she was standing next to her mother's bedside, hand on her cool cheek and frantically whispered words begging her mother not to leave her. Not when they'd been so close to having everything back to the way it should be.

The memory faded, replaced by the sparkling chandeliers brightening *La Reina*'s halls. Just as she had that morning so many years ago, she drew up, drawing strength from some inner source as she locked her emotions away where they couldn't betray her. She backed away and walked back to the ballroom, her footsteps thankfully muffled by the thick carpet.

This was why she'd kept the walls around her heart, why love and marriage had never been an option after Mom's death. Because the brief, exquisite happiness she'd found this past week made the fall so much worse.

Her initial fear had been accurate. She'd fallen into the same trap as her mother, drawn in by a handsome face and charming words, dreaming of forever when she'd only been a fleeting interest, a novelty in his glitzy world. She'd thought he'd truly wanted her. The baby. After yesterday...a life. Together.

But he'd stayed silent. Alejandro, the man who always had a snappy comeback or a witty comment at the ready, had stayed silent. She'd heard his answer in that silence, loud and clear.

At least, she consoled herself as she moved around the room, she'd found out before she did something stupid like confess her feelings to him. She would be strong. Stronger than her mother. Stronger than the weak woman she'd allowed herself to be this past week. A temporary lapse. But one that tonight, after the party, she would rectify.

After another round of the ballroom, a few words of direction to a slightly harried-looking server and a check-in with her assistant later, Alejandro reentered.

His gaze landed on her. The cracks in her heart ripped open.

He came up to her, eyes blank, face devoid of a smile.

"I'd like to speak with you after the party." The smallest glimmer came into his eyes. "The board voted unanimously to support *La Reina*."

Somehow she smiled and forced herself to reach out, pat him on the arm. "Congratulations."

He leaned down, kissed her cheek and moved away toward a group of older gentlemen. She barely stopped herself from reaching up to the touch the spot where his lips had brushed. The light caress had been casual, like a kiss you might give a friend you hadn't seen in a while. Not a woman you loved.

The final confirmation, like a dagger to the heart.

The next three hours passed agonizingly slowly. But

finally the last guest left, the band started to pack up and Suzie's students began to clear the tables.

Alejandro appeared by her side.

"Ready to go home?"

"Yes." More than ready. She never wanted to set foot in France again. It would be too painful.

He held out an arm. She took it, her fingers settling on his sleeve, and allowed him to escort her down the elegant hallway of the ship. A ship she'd come to care about, to see as a grand old lady getting a second chance at life.

Another loss. Another reason why forming emotional attachments was such a bad idea.

The drive back to the villa was silent. Unlike the comfort of yesterday's drive back from Provence, this one was fraught with tension. Alejandro either ignored her cool detachment or was too consumed by his own thoughts to notice.

No matter, she reassured herself. She didn't need him. Not anymore.

He pulled up in front of the villa, the white stairs glowing in the moonlight. He got out, came round before she had her seat belt unbuckled and opened the door for her.

"Home."

She breathed in. "No. It's not."

Her words hung in the stillness of the night as Alejandro's attention suddenly riveted on her.

"What?"

"I heard what you and your father were talking about."

How had everything gone so wrong so quickly? Alejandro rubbed the bridge of his nose. Four hours ago he'd been in love, his certainty in the success of the first project that was truly his allowing him to entertain thoughts of shopping for a ring for the mother of his child.

And then his father, with surprisingly good intentions, had once again taken his life and turned it on its head.

"You don't think you're capable, do you? Of being a father, of…" Her voice trailed off, choked with emotion. He moved forward, to hold her close like he had at the inn, but she held up a hand. "Of committing," she finished.

It was all happening at once. Too much. Too much swirling around inside like a hurricane, destroying everything in its path. He'd built his life around what his father had done, had pursued women and notoriety to punish him.

Except it had been a mistake. One mistake committed out of pain instead of a calculated affair. He'd lived nearly twenty years of his life on a myth that he'd been too angry, too hurt, to examine more closely. To act like an adult and talk with his father.

His entire reality had been called into question in one conversation. Much as he wanted to blame his father—how much easier that would have been—he had no one to blame but himself. And Javier's words of warning had made him wonder…did he really want to be a father? A husband? Or was this just another twisted trick of his psyche?

He didn't have an answer. Which was probably an answer in itself.

"Calandra…if you heard everything…" He spread his hands helplessly. "I don't know what to think."

He watched whatever they'd had end as her shoulders straightened, her chin came up and her mask slid back into place, all within a few seconds. His heart, his chest, his whole damn body ached to hold her, to erase the last few hours and recapture the magic they'd found in Provence.

But he kept his hands by his sides. He'd borne witness to the painful price her parents' abandonment had demanded of Calandra. How could he risk doing the same thing to the baby? Risk putting Calandra through yet another rejection? Like his father had said, if he didn't know one hundred percent that he wanted this, it was better to let her go. Let their child go.

"It seems, then, that I have my answer." A heartbeat where she hesitated, where the ice in her eyes cracked and revealed the insurmountable pain he'd caused her. Even if he did find an answer, he'd never be able to come back from this. From hurting her so deeply.

"Goodbye, Señor Cabrera."

Somehow, he thought as he watched her walk up the stairs and disappear into the villa, he'd always known Calandra Smythe would walk out of his life.

He'd just had no idea he'd be the one to drive her away.

CHAPTER TWENTY-ONE

Three weeks later

SILVER MOONLIGHT CREATED a mystical glow on the ocean, the waves rising and falling beneath a dark sky speckled with stars. Calandra sat on the beach, one hand draped across her belly.

The ocean had looked incredible from the porch, the muffled roar calling to her. The view from her attic bedroom was nothing compared to the beauty laid out before her. Waves crashed on a smooth beach, the white-capped peaks glowing in the moonlight, the water tumbling over itself in frothy splendor to almost kiss her bare feet before receding. Stars spiraled above her head.

She kept her eyes on the barest glint of a horizon, where the midnight blue of the sky met the even darker blue of the ocean. Beneath her fingertips, something fluttered.

A sad smile tugged at her lips. She'd felt it this morning, the briefest twinge. She'd chalked it up to muscle spasms. But the fluttering had grown stronger, until it had been impossible to deny that she was feeling her baby move inside her for the first time.

Johanna had insisted on baking a cake to celebrate the occasion. A yellow cake frosted with caramel and topped off with sprinkles in the shape of baby rattles she'd served after dinner.

For all the years that Calandra had spent taking care of Johanna, her sister had repaid the favor twice over in the three weeks Calandra had been home. She'd picked her up at the airport, held her while she forced out the whole story on the couch with thankfully minimal tears. She'd arranged a meeting for Calandra with a finance student from her college to help her decide how best to manage the five-hundred-thousand-dollar deposit that had appeared in her account twenty-four hours after she'd left Marseille.

An email had also been sent with an attachment, a formal letter of recommendation from Alejandro Cabrera himself, head of Cabrera Shipping.

Last week she'd been mindlessly flipping through late-night movies, unable to sleep, when *The Scarlet Pimpernel* had come on. She'd changed the channel with a savage push of a button, then changed it back again. Landing on the scene where the beautiful, tortured Marguerite had looked at Percy with sad eyes and whispered, "This is some absurd role you're playing. I don't know why. But I'm sure it is. Perhaps to keep the world at a distance. Only now you're shutting me out as well," it had plunged a knife into her heart so deep it had made her eyes burn.

She'd done the right thing. He hadn't been playing a role when he'd flat-out told her he didn't know if he wanted her in his life, wanted their child in his life. A definitive answer. One that had nearly killed her.

Better to know now, before the baby came and could

get attached to a father who would disappear from its life, than to suffer that heartache later.

It didn't stop the wondering. Or the memories. The dreadful, horrid, wonderful memories of a week when she'd climbed the Eiffel Tower, seen the Mediterranean from the deck of a yacht and knelt down to smell a sprig of lavender in front of a historic abbey.

At least Alejandro had given her that, she consoled herself. She'd lived more in the past week than she had in years. That little taste of life had come just in time. When their—her, she corrected herself—her child arrived, she would make sure it got that same taste of life, that same joy in both the big and small.

And through that, her child would at least know their father a little.

A breeze blew in, bringing with it the scent of sea salt. Out of the corner of her eye, something appeared. She turned her head and gasped. A yacht glided across the water, elegant and glowing white under the kiss of moonlight. If she squinted, she could just make out letters written in graceful red cursive.

Her heart thudded. It wasn't possible. She was imagining things. Or hallucinating.

The yacht stilled, bobbing gently up and down on the waves. She pushed to her feet, eyes trained on the boat as her heart pounded in her throat. Was it him? Did she want it to be him? After nearly a month of silence—no texts, no phone calls, no letters—what was left to be said?

A shape appeared out of the ocean, a ghost emerging from the water. She took a few steps back, fear mixing in with her adrenaline.

"Kitty Hawk's nice this time of year."

The husky voice echoed up over the beach. Her

mouth dropped open as Alejandro walked out of the water, white shirt clinging like a second skin to his muscular chest, black pants pasted to his legs. With dark curls plastered to his forehead and that wicked grin flashing in the dark, he looked like a hero from one of her old paperback romances.

"You're wet."

His laughter, deep and rich, chased away the chill that had settled on her skin when she'd first seen the yacht.

"Nothing gets by you, does it?"

"Rarely." She crossed her arms over her middle, partly out of instinct to protect the baby now fluttering wildly in her stomach, and partly to keep herself from running down the beach and throwing herself into his arms. "Once in a while, though, I've been known to make a mistake."

The barb hit home. His grin faded as he smoothed the wet hair out of his face.

"So have I. In fact, I made a big one pretty recently."

"Aside from swimming in the Atlantic at night?"

"Yeah." He took a step toward her. She didn't move. She wouldn't back down. "I let the woman I love walk away."

Love. That word echoed in her head, over and over again. She wanted to reach out, grab it, hug it to her chest. He loved her?

Don't. Don't let him in.

"Hmm."

"Hmm," he repeated. "As in, 'hmm, I like what I'm hearing' or 'hmm, go jump in the ocean, you bastard'?"

"I haven't heard enough to make a decision." Her

eyes slid back to the yacht. "Seriously, why did you jump in the ocean?"

"I wasn't planning on it." He gestured at his soaking-wet clothes. "Believe me, I wouldn't have worn this to go swimming. I planned on mooring the boat, coming ashore via the dinghy and kidnapping you. Unfortunately, I haven't taken it out by myself in quite some time." He gestured at the dark waves. "It's now a permanent addition to the bottom of the Atlantic. But I'm a good swimmer, and that's not important. What is important is I need…" Even at this distance, she could see, *feel*, the intensity of his gaze sharpen as he stared at her like they'd been parted for years instead of just a few weeks.

"I need you, Calandra."

Hadn't she just been ruminating on how she hadn't really been living her life? Had let fear mask itself as discipline and kept herself emotionally distant from everyone and everything? Alejandro was offering her the chance to break free from the past.

"You were going to kidnap me?" she finally asked.

"Romantically kidnap you. With your permission, of course."

Damn her lips for twitching. She'd missed him. His humor. His charm. The way he looked at her like she was the only one in the world. But she'd allowed herself to be suckered in once. To open her heart and believe he could be different. Would it be fear to reject him, or practicality?

"Do you still feel about me the way you did when we left Provence?"

Her mouth dried up as heat blossomed inside her. "What do you mean?"

"You know exactly what I mean, Calandra. I saw it in your eyes. I know what you were going to tell me the night of the party."

"You said we both had our answer. Nothing more needs to be said."

Long strides ate up the distance between them. She stood, frozen in place by desire and want and the dread that if she moved a muscle she'd break down, throw her arms around his neck and ask him to never leave again.

"Much more needs to be said." He laid a hand on her cheek, the gesture so gentle and tender it brought a lump to her throat. "For starters, I am not like my father."

He sucked in a deep breath as he savored the feel of her skin. He'd been an idiot to wait as long as he had to come for her. But it had taken the past three weeks and several long, difficult conversations with his father, his mother, Adrian and even Everleigh to make him see sense.

"Do something incredibly romantic," Everleigh had encouraged.

So he'd ordered *The Scarlet Pimpernel* to make the crossing from Marseille to Kitty Hawk, North Carolina, and moor right in front of her aunt Norine's ramshackle beachfront cottage. A storm had slowed their journey by a few hours so that instead of arriving just before sunset as he'd planned, they'd sailed in under the light of the moon. His captain had tried to discourage him from taking the dinghy out with the waves as high as they were, had offered to take the yacht to the nearest marina and call Alejandro a car. But the marina was an hour away by boat, and he hadn't wanted to wait.

His pride smarted a little from getting tossed into the ocean. He'd envisioned striding up the beach with the confidence and swagger of Douglas Fairbanks, not a drowned rat. But it had been worth it to reach Calandra as soon as he could.

God, she was beautiful. Dark hair flowing past her shoulders, arms crossed over her belly, now slightly rounded and peeking out from beneath the hem of her shirt. The need to hold her, cradle her stomach and the life growing inside her, feel her curl into his body the way she had all those nights ago, almost overpowered him.

First things first. Apology. Explanation. More apology.

"I'm so sorry, Calandra." He placed his forehead against hers, exhaled sharply when she didn't pull away. Even if she pushed him into the ocean and told him she never wanted to see him again, he would savor every touch she allowed him. "That night on *La Reina*, what you overheard was the first time my father and I have had a conversation about anything other than my behavior or business. He told me things about his affair that put it in a very different light. That rendered most of my life obsolete."

Calandra leaned back and his stomach dropped.

"I don't understand."

"I lived most of my life, my flings, my ability to remain unattached, my exploits, to punish my father." He closed his eyes for a moment. "Only to find out that my entire existence was built on a misunderstanding. An assumption I made that turned out not to be true. Suddenly..." He raked a hand through his hair. "I had no idea who I was. I was faced with nearly twenty years of distance and foolish decisions and a persona I'd concocted that wasn't really me. It made me question everything. Including whether I was pursuing you and being a father for the right reasons."

He waited for the shutter to drop down, for her beautiful, misty eyes to turn steely gray and her voice to whip out an order to leave and never come back.

Hope bloomed, tiny but fierce, as she stayed put, continued to look at him thoughtfully instead of with the disgust and fury he'd anticipated.

"So what did you decide?"

He barely resisted kissing her for uttering her question in that prim, controlled voice that drove him crazy. Crazy because he admired her, how she managed to lead and coordinate and do all the amazing things she did for her career. Crazy, too, because he wanted to kiss her senseless until the primness was replaced by that breathy moan that set his blood on fire.

"Cabrera Shipping became the first thing I really wanted in life for me. Making it a success because I wanted to build something. *La Reina* was the second, and the first thing that was truly my own. I never thought anything could be more important than *La Reina*."

He reached out, slowly, giving her plenty of time to back up, before he placed his hand on her belly. She didn't lean into him, but she didn't pull away. He knelt down in the sand, gave in to temptation and placed the softest of kisses on her stomach.

"You, and our child, are more important to me than anything in the world, Calandra." He looked up at her, letting every emotion he'd repressed show. If he lost, at least he'd know he gave it his all. "It started out with me wanting more purpose in my life. The chance to be the father mine had never been. And then I realized that it wasn't just our child, but you that I wanted, too. The woman I've been falling in love with for the past three years."

A tear traced its way down her face, leaving behind a trail on her cheek that glistened in the silver light. He stood and hurriedly wiped it away.

"Calandra, I—"

"I'm sorry!" she cried out and flung her arms around his neck. He hesitated for half a second before wrapping his arms around her waist and hauling her against him, burying his face in her hair and breathing her in.

"You have nothing to be sorry for," he whispered in her ear as he cradled her in his arms.

"But I do." She pulled back to look him in the eye, her hands settling on his cheeks. "I heard enough of your conversation with your father to know how serious it was. You told me about your relationship with him, how tumultuous it was, but I focused on the little bit I heard and made it all about me and my past." She wiped away more tears with the back of her hand. "I should have given you grace. I should have trusted you and told you how much I respect your drive, your dedication…how much I loved you. And instead I assumed the worst and I ran."

He cradled her face in his hands and kissed the tears from her cheeks as joy filled him, true joy like he'd never known before.

"I'm not perfect, Calandra."

A smile broke through her tears. "Trust me, I know."

"Minx." He kissed the tip of her nose. "I mean that I'm just starting to get to know myself. It's going to take a while. There will be days I struggle. It's a lot to ask anyone to take on. Selfish, really."

"And I'm just starting to confront my past," Calandra said as she laid her hands on top of his. "I have trust issues. Big ones. I buried myself in routines and checklists and a job that required order. I struggle to share my emotions. I have a lot to deal with regarding my parents."

"Well…" So much. So much pain on both sides. "Aren't we a pair?"

Her eyes dimmed a fraction. "Do you think…"

"I think," he replied as her voice trailed off, "that we both love each other. That we know each other better than anyone else does. And," he added as he placed a hand on her stomach once more, "that that's enough for a new start. I want to marry you, Calandra. I want to wake up to your face the rest of my life, to our baby in the nursery. I want you to drag me to little culinary schools and remind me that I'm being an ass and not let me get away with anything."

A wobbly smile crossed her face as more tears spilled down her cheeks.

"Was that a proposal?"

He dropped back down on one knee and grabbed both her hands in his. "A horrible one, but yes. Let me try that again. Calandra Smythe, love of my life, will you marry me?"

With her breathy "yes" echoing in his ears, he surged to his feet, swept her into his arms and kissed her beneath a sea of stars.

* * * * *

If you fell in love with
Proof of Their One Hot Night
you're sure to love the first installment of
The Infamous Cabrera Brothers trilogy,
His Billion-Dollar Takeover Temptation*!*
And be sure to check out Emmy Grayson's
next story!

* * *

#3953 HIS MAJESTY'S HIDDEN HEIR
Princesses by Royal Decree
by Lucy Monroe
Prince Konstantin can't forget Emma Carmichael, the woman who vanished after royal pressure forced him to end their relationship. A surprise meeting five years later shocks Konstantin: Emma has a son. Unmistakably *his* son. And now he'll claim them both!

#3954 THE GREEK'S CINDERELLA DEAL
Cinderellas of Convenience
by Carol Marinelli
When tycoon Costa declares he'll hire Mary if she attends a party with him, she's dazed—by his generosity and their outrageous attraction! And as the clock strikes midnight on their deal, Cinderella unravels—in the Greek's bed...

#3955 PREGNANT AFTER ONE FORBIDDEN NIGHT
The Queen's Guard
by Marcella Bell
Innocent royal guard Jenna has never been tempted away from duty. She's never been tempted by a man before! Until her forbidden night with notoriously untamable billionaire Sebastian, which ends with her carrying his baby!

#3956 THE BRIDE HE STOLE FOR CHRISTMAS
by Caitlin Crews
Hours before the woman he can't forget walks down the aisle, Crete steals Timoney back! And now he has the night before Christmas to prove to them both that he won't break her heart all over again...

#3957 BOUND BY HER SHOCKING SECRET
by Abby Green

It takes all of Mia's courage to tell tycoon Daniel about their daughter. Though tragedy tore them apart, he deserves to know he's a father. But accepting his proposal? That will require something far more extraordinary...

#3958 CONFESSIONS OF HIS CHRISTMAS HOUSEKEEPER
by Sharon Kendrick

Stunned when an accident leaves her estranged husband, Giacomo, unable to remember their year-long marriage, Louise becomes his temporary housekeeper. She'll spend Christmas helping him regain his memory. But dare she confess the explosive feelings she still has for him?

#3959 UNWRAPPED BY HER ITALIAN BOSS
Christmas with a Billionaire
by Michelle Smart

After a rocky first impression, innocent Meredith's got a lot to prove to her new billionaire boss, Giovanni! He's trusting her to make his opulent train's maiden voyage a success. Trusting herself around him? That's another challenge entirely...

#3960 THE BILLIONAIRE'S PROPOSITION IN PARIS
Secrets of Billionaire Siblings
by Heidi Rice

By hiring event planner Katherine and inviting her to a lavish Paris ball, Connall plans to find out all he needs to take revenge on her half brother. He's not counting on their ever-building electricity to bring him to his knees!

_____